The

CW00879953

The Twins' New Neighbor

Katrina Kahler

Table of Contents

CHAPTER ONE

Alexa

A wildfire had erupted in bushland a few miles away, and we were all on edge. When a pounding knock sounded on the front door, I rushed to open it. Behind the agitated firefighter, the sky was filled with an orange glow, and thick smoke filled the air.

"The fire's headed this way, and you need to leave now!" the man yelled at my uncle, who had appeared behind me. "Grab your kids and any pets and get out. If you have nowhere else to go, there's an evacuation center being set up at the community hall on the other side of town."

Aunt Beth hurried over to us, her face crumpling. "Can we pack a bag?"

"No!" The firefighter's abrupt retort made her jump. "This area is under serious threat. We're evacuating everyone."

Outside, we saw a police car driving slowly by. A commanding voice sounded through a megaphone. "You must evacuate! All residents need to leave the area immediately. You must evacuate. Evacuation center at the town community hall. Everyone evacuate immediately!" The words were repeated over and over as the car patrolled the streets.

"Come on!" my uncle urged Aunt Beth. "We have to go!" He reached for the car keys that were sitting on the hallway sideboard and tugged on my younger brother's arm, shuffling him out the door. "Tyler, move!"

My brother turned to me in horror.

"It'll be okay, Tyler," I tried to assure him.

"I'm sorry," he mumbled.

I had no idea what he was apologizing for, but there was no time to question him further.

"Come on! Come on!" Uncle Vern's panicked voice urged us. "Get in the car!"

As I followed them outside, I looked over the fence to see Ali, my neighbor, running to the car parked in the driveway. The engine was running, and the rest of her family were seated in the car, waiting for her. She locked eyes with me for a fraction of a second before climbing inside.

"Alexa, get in the car!" My uncle's frantic tone pushed me to do as he asked.

Closing the door behind me, I buckled my seatbelt as he reversed sharply onto the street, almost colliding with the neighbors' four-wheel drive. A squeal of brakes added to the tension, and I turned to see Ali, her sister, Casey, and their younger brother, Lucas, in the rear seat. Ali sat next to the window, and her mouth was agape as she stared back at me. The worry in her expression mirrored the fear that was sitting like a heavy lump in the pit of my stomach.

With an abrupt jerk of the gears, Uncle Vern sped past their car and accelerated along the street. As he drove, I stared at the blazing flames that were licking at the dry section of bushland bordering that part of the road.

I watched in horror as a ball of fire bounced across the street and onto the rooftop of a two-story home, causing it to burst into flame. Two firefighters rushed to hose the house down. If the fire couldn't be stopped, my aunt and uncle's house, the place where my brother and I had taken refuge just two weeks previously, would be in its path. Would their house still be there when we returned?

Tyler's hand clung to mine on the seat beside me. Terror filled his eyes, and I tightened my grip to reassure not only him but myself as well. My aunt was hysterical in the front seat while Uncle Vern tried to calm her. Dodging a fireball that skipped across the road right in front of us, he maneuvered the car with an erratic turn of the steering wheel, causing Tyler to be thrown against me.

I'd heard stories where people were caught in firestorms and failed to survive. At the time, the stories were news reports on the TV. They involved people I didn't know, and while the scenes were horrific, for me, there was no personal attachment. This time, Tyler and I were in the thick of it all. And it was terrifying.

If all the houses in our street caught fire and became a pile of burned rubble, what would happen to us then?

CHAPTER TWO

Casey
Two Weeks Earlier

When I woke that Saturday morning, I had no idea of the upcoming events that would change my world. The sun was shining brightly outside, we had the weekend to look forward to, and all I could hear was the sound of my twin sister's breathing. We had both slept late, and Ali was still asleep in her bed alongside mine. Her lips twitched slightly, and I wondered if she might still be dreaming. I'd heard the murmur of her voice during the night. I wasn't able to make out what she was saying, and I wondered if she'd remember her dream when she awoke.

I was still adjusting to my new life in Ali's house, the house I was yet to refer to as my own. While the spacious bedroom that I shared with my twin allowed plenty of room for all the new additions… an extra bed, an extra bedside table, and an extra desk, each of them matching the ones that were previously in place for Ali, sharing a room was something new for both of us. Except for occasional sleepovers and summer camp, we'd always had our own private space. Since our parents' marriage, however, my life had taken on a whole new perspective, and I hadn't been prepared for the whirlwind that came with it.

I thought back to the very second I first laid eyes on my twin… when she walked into my classroom, and I discovered she had my face, it was life-changing, not only for me but for Ali as well. We soon discovered we were twins who had been separated at birth. Our mom decided she could only keep one of us and by a twist of fate, Ali was the one to be adopted by another family. From that second on, we were unaware of the other's existence. Until fate brought us together again and everything changed.

Once the secret was out, Ali and I gradually became more than sisters. We also became best friends. After the tragic death of Ali's adopted mother, time passed by with us plotting and planning in the hope that Ali's dad, Chris, would fall in love with our birth mom so we could become a real family. Eventually, a fairy tale wedding took place, one that included all the trimmings. Our mother was such a beautiful bride, and when she and Chris said the words, "I do," it was magical.

As I lay in bed that morning, enjoying not having to get up for school, I focused on the array of photo frames spread across the bookshelf on the far wall. The image of Ali and me in our flower girl gowns, with bouquets in hand and our hair sparkling with glitter, was an instant reminder of the special day we had celebrated together.

It was followed by a romantic honeymoon for our parents in Tahiti. Tahiti, of all places!

Chris didn't spare any expense and chose a private bungalow on an isolated palm-fringed beach with a personal chef and a lagoon-style pool. Suntanned and glowing, Mom and Chris had beamed at the camera, and it was easy to see how happy they both were in the pics they sent us. Ali and I had selected one of our favorites and placed it in a frame, alongside all our other special photos.

It was all so romantic, and I wondered if I'd ever get the chance to experience something so special. While our parents were away, Grandma Ann came to stay with us, and the reality of our new life hit with a bang. Grandma Ann's strict rules about bedtime and behavior were non-negotiable, and we found ourselves wishing our parents would hurry and return home.

We became a blended family, living under the same roof. The luxury that had once been Ali's to enjoy alone with her dad, now also belonged to Mom, Lucas, and me. While Ali was happy to share each and every aspect and continued to remind me that the house wasn't just hers, it was in fact, *ours*, I found it difficult to take that idea on board.

As the weeks passed, Lucas began to act out. Although he had always been annoying, he was becoming worse than ever. Mom kept saying it was an adjustment period. He wasn't used to sharing his mother with a new stepdad and was probably trying to get her attention.

Whatever the cause, I wished he would stop.

During the transition, my twin and I also encountered our ups and downs, and these were still ongoing. Just the night before, we were involved in a disagreement of sorts, something that was happening more frequently as time went by. Sometimes I wondered if Ali might prefer the way things were, where she had a bedroom to herself, and no in-house siblings to deal with. The constant attempts by Lucas to barge into our room and invade our space affected Ali as well as me, and I was forced to remind myself that her life had been turned upside down too. Even so, I had thought that once we began living together as a family, my twin and I would become closer. But so far, that hadn't happened at all.

There were so many adjustments, and in addition to all the changes, there was one that continued to catch me off guard.

"We're a family now," Mom insisted before the wedding. "We should all have the same last name."

Because Jackie Jackson sounded funny, Mom had discussed keeping our old name, Wrigley. But she and Chris eventually decided we should have the same name as Chris and Ali and be fully united. They'd even arranged for updated birth certificates for Lucas and me, a lengthy process, requiring a legal name change first.

It felt strange when I pinned my new school captain badge to my jacket or sweater each morning, and my name stared back. My twin and I now shared not only the same face and the same house, but we also shared the same last name. It was the final tie to link us together.

Hopefully, over time, the settling in problems would no longer be such an issue. Then Ali and I could go back to being the close twins we had been not so long ago. The thoughts filled my head as I sat up in bed. So much had happened in such a short period, and I was still trying to process it all.

Alerted by the sound of a car door closing outside the window by my bed, I looked out to see that our neighbor, Mr. Johnson, had just pulled into his driveway. I watched as the rear passenger door opened, and a young girl around my age stepped out, clutching tightly to a bulging plastic bag full of belongings. A younger boy climbed out and stood alongside her. The pair surveyed their surroundings as Mr. Johnson reached into the trunk and retrieved a suitcase. He nodded at the hesitant pair and signaled for them to follow him. As the girl walked, some of the contents spilled out of the bag she was carrying. Nudging the boy, she indicated the clothes on the ground.

Half-hidden by the curtain, I watched the scene unfold, and when the girl suddenly looked up in my direction, I was able to take in her features. Turning abruptly away, she hurried after Mr. Johnson to the front door, leaving the boy to collect the trail of items that had fallen in her wake.

Mr. and Mrs. Johnson didn't have any children of their own, which caused me to wonder who the kids were. According to Chris, who I had to keep remembering was now my stepdad, the Johnsons had high-paying corporate jobs and worked long hours, so they were rarely at home.

By the look of the suitcase and the other belongings, the new arrivals were staying for a while. The question was, for how long?

With my curiosity spiking, I jumped out of bed and went to the bathroom to shower and change. Mom and Chris had very little to do with the Johnsons, but they might have some information to share.

At that point in time, I was unaware of what was ahead. My life had already been turned full circle, but the two arrivals next door would cause an impact so far-reaching if I'd been forewarned, I would never have believed it.

CHAPTER THREE

Alexa

When we turned into the driveway where my aunt and uncle lived, I stared in awe at the immaculate house in front of us. It was different in every way imaginable to the trailer we had left behind. An anxious knot gripped tightly to my stomach and wouldn't let go. It had been there from the minute my uncle arrived to collect us earlier that morning. The trailer park where my brother and I had lived for as long as I could remember had been our home. It was what we were used to.

Then, in the blink of an eye, Tyler and I were shuffled with our meager belongings into our uncle's car, while our mother waved a quick goodbye. The distraught look on my brother's face as he stared out the rear window had ripped at my heartstrings. How could our mom have let this happen? It was impossible to comprehend.

The eviction notice had arrived a week earlier. After months of unpaid rent, the manager of the trailer park wanted us out. "You've had enough chances, Charlene," he grumbled at Mom as he handed her the notice. "I'm sorry, but you can't keep living here for free. You can have two weeks to find another place, and then you have to leave."

Word spread and the Child Protective Services Department, who had been keeping a regular eye on our situation for quite some time, stepped in. A court order arrived two days later, advising that Tyler and I would be taken into foster care if our mother couldn't find a suitable living arrangement. With no one else to call on, Mom decided to contact her sister and beg for help.

We had only met our aunt once before, and it wasn't a

fond memory at all. At the time, she had been passing through the area where we lived and decided to swing by and see us. I don't know what prompted the sudden urge to visit. Perhaps it was curiosity, as she claimed, or maybe there was guilt involved. I couldn't be sure of the real reason, but the look of distaste when she stepped inside our trailer was etched on my memory.

Regarding Mom with a disdainful look, she shook her head as she spoke. "Seriously, Charlene, how on earth do you live like this?"

She hadn't seen her sister in years, but her first words were filled with scorn. I disliked her immediately.

"Good to see you too, Beth." My mom's sarcasm wasn't lost on me. "What are you doing here, anyway?"

"Just checking you're still alive. Though I have no idea how, when you live in conditions like this."

"Not everyone is lucky enough to marry a millionaire," Mom scoffed, glancing out the door to where a man was seated in his car. "Is he too good to come in and meet his niece and nephew?"

My aunt dismissed Mom's remark with a wave of her hand. "Vern has a deadline to make, and we're in a hurry. I just wanted to check in on you. You could pretend you're pleased to see me."

Mom raised her eyebrows and huffed. "Well, we're still here."

The woman who I had just learned was my aunt turned away from her sister with a shake of her head and focused on me instead. Her eyes traveled down to my feet and back again. "So, this must be Alexa. Hello, Alexa. I'm your Aunt Beth."

"Hello," I mumbled and slumped back in my chair.

Her eyes then flickered to Tyler, who was seated beside me. "And you must be...?"

Tyler regarded her with a frown and didn't respond.

"His name's Tyler," I answered for him.

"Oh, that's right, Tyler. Hello, Tyler, how are you?"

"Good," he said, his brown eyes taking in the stranger.

"Good, thank you!" Mom scowled at him. "Remember your manners."

If there was one thing my mother did demand, it was the words, please and thank you. As long as we remembered those, she pretty much left us to our own devices.

"I'd offer you a coffee, Beth, but we're out of milk. And I know you won't drink it without," Mom said, attempting to be civil.

"Thanks, but I don't have time to hang around. I just wanted to check up on you. Nothing's changed, I see." My aunt turned to me and lifted her eyebrows. "Nice to meet you, Alexa. And you too, Tyler," she said, almost as an afterthought.

13

Dropping a business card on the counter, she pointed to it. "You can reach me on that number, Charlene. Give me a call sometime."

Mom gave the card a passing glance before looking back at her sister. "See ya around, *sis*." She emphasized the final word as our aunt stepped out the door.

I watched as her high heels connected with the rickety step, and I silently wished she would stumble and fall. It would serve her right for being so rude.

She walked around to the other side of the expensive-looking car, pulled the door open, and stepped inside. Her husband lifted his hand in a brief wave then accelerated away as if he couldn't escape the trailer park quickly enough.

That was the only memory I had of my aunt and uncle. And then, several years later, after a desperate phone call from my mother, begging for them to take us in, I found myself in the driveway of their home alongside my brother. Our possessions consisted of a tattered old suitcase and a trash bag to store the remainder of our clothes. We had been uprooted from all we had ever known, and the knot inside me clenched even tighter as I stepped out of the car and onto the pavement.

Clutching firmly to the plastic bag, I held it in front of me like a security blanket, something to cling to for protection. I sucked in a breath and looked at my uncle, who gave me an encouraging smile. It helped to ease the tension a little, and I forced my feet to follow behind him.

As I walked, the cheap plastic bag I was holding gave way, and several items fell onto the ground. As I attempted to gather the bundle together, I turned to my brother and hissed quietly, "Tyler, pick that stuff up." I then darted a nervous look at the front door, hoping my aunt wouldn't suddenly appear and see the assortment of clothing scattered across her pavement.

My gaze wandered to the top floor of the neighboring

property. I'm not sure what pulled my eyes in that direction, perhaps I sensed I was being watched. Squinting against the morning sunlight, I blinked and spotted a girl peering from an upper window. Embarrassed by the pile of clothes that Tyler was still trying to collect, I quickly hurried after my uncle, swallowing the lump in my throat as I walked.

I had already promised myself that I wouldn't cry, at least for Tyler's sake. I was his older sister, and I needed to be strong. At the sight of my aunt standing in the doorway, however, I felt my lips tremble.

"It'll just be for a little while," my mother had promised Uncle Vern that morning. "Just until I get a job and can find somewhere else to live."

I'd heard Mom promise to find work on so many occasions that I'd lost count. Forced to survive on welfare payments, we had barely made ends meet. With our mother's compulsive gambling habits, there was rarely any money left to spend on food or clothes. Her habits were so ingrained that I couldn't see her changing any time soon. With that in mind, I wasn't holding my breath for her to get her life together so she could take us back.

As I approached my aunt, I could easily see by her expression that we weren't welcome. So why did she agree to take us in? Was it because of obligation, or was it guilt? I knew I should be grateful, but her lack of warmth was making that very difficult.

I hated being a charity case. And I hated the idea of being lumbered with people who didn't want us. They were our relatives, but they didn't even know us. Although Uncle Vern had done his best to be welcoming, our aunt's icy demeanor cut through to my soul.

Deep down, I suspected my mother had been glad to see us go. My brother and I were an unwanted burden, and she had complained several times over the years. "My life would be so much easier if I didn't have kids. If I didn't have kids, I could do this. If I didn't have kids, I could have done that." I'd often heard her moaning to the other trailer park residents. Tyler heard every word, as well.

I was aware of the expression, 'Be careful what you wish for!'

Mom had certainly been given her wish. She no longer had her kids weighing her down. But as well as her kids, she had lost her home. It was a crumby old trailer, but we'd called it 'home.'

Perhaps it was her karma for wishing to be rid of us.

Now we were faced with strangers who didn't want us either.

For Tyler and me, our future was a black hole, and we had no idea what was ahead, or where we would end up.

In the meantime, we had to stick together, and I was determined not to let anyone tear us apart.

CHAPTER FOUR

Ali

When Casey told me about the new arrivals, I was as curious as my twin, and I jumped out of bed, quickly got dressed and hurried down the stairs. Dad had spoken to Mr. and Mrs. Johnson a few times previously, and I had met them a while back. But apart from an occasional wave over the fence, we'd had very little contact. Mr. Johnson was quite friendly, though Mrs. Johnson kept to herself.

I wanted to learn more about their visitors, especially as, according to Casey, the girl looked similar in age to us. As well, I wondered if the boy could be a playmate for Lucas, which might get him out of our hair. While I loved my brother, Lucas had become unbearable. His constant demand for attention was driving me crazy and putting my nerves on edge.

My twin was quite comfortable in telling him to leave our room, and she had even slammed the door in his face on a few occasions. As the weeks went by, I started to mimic her actions. It was the only thing that worked. Before that, I was the "good" twin, while Casey was the "evil" one. That was how Lucas referred to us. Because he thought I was on his side, he figured he was welcome to join in with whatever we were doing.

But Casey didn't hold back. "Go away, Lucas!" she exclaimed over and over again.

Lucas would turn to me, expecting me to defend him. At first, I felt sorry for him and did exactly that, but I soon toughened up. The next time our door flung open, it was me saying the words, "Lucas! Out of our room. Now!"

Taken aback, he looked at me, stunned. The first time,

I was overwhelmed with guilt. But when I saw the shake of Casey's head, I gave Lucas a gentle shove out into the hallway. "I'll play a game with you later, okay?" I whispered then shut the door behind him. That response led to more annoying antics, and I learned not to encourage him at all.

In the beginning, I loved having my siblings and my birth mom living permanently with Dad and me. We were one big family, and the house had become their home as well as mine. I'd grown used to calling Jackie, Mom. So much so that I never referred to her as Jackie anymore. Lucas had quickly settled in, and his toys were constantly scattered all over the place. At first, I didn't mind. It was all very new and exciting and fun — no more only child syndrome for me as I always had someone to hang out with.

Sharing my room with Casey was exactly as I had imagined it would be. It was a thrill to set up a matching bed, a bedside table, and a desk on opposite sides of the room. It felt like summer camp all over again. I made some space in the closet and cleared some shelves, as well as a bathroom drawer so Casey could store her belongings. She didn't own too many clothes, so there was plenty of room, and as we had done in the past, we continued to share absolutely everything.

As the weeks passed, though, the novelty began to wear off. Our bedroom felt cluttered and cramped, and I longed for my own space again. Casey wasn't a neat freak like me, and her side was littered with clothes, shoes, books, and a myriad of other belongings. I knew I shouldn't let it bother me, but I couldn't help it.

Each time I opened my closet, the difference in our habits hit me with a thud. My dad had called me OCD in the past. An obsessive-compulsive disorder was something we joked about, but it was just the way I was. My side of the closet was immaculately organized whereas Casey's clothes were often tossed into messy piles on the shelves. It was no wonder she had trouble finding the things she needed.

As well, I was frustrated by my lack of private space. I mentioned this to Dad when we had some rare alone time together. He said he understood, but I didn't think that was the case at all.

"Just give it some time, Ali," he said with an encouraging smile. "It's an adjustment for all of us, and I'm sure it's just as hard for Casey as it is for you. Try to be a little more considerate."

More considerate? What was that supposed to mean? Were Casey's needs more important than mine?

"Casey's so easy-going," I overheard him say to Mom. "I wish Ali would lighten up sometimes. She takes things much too seriously."

What was he implying? Was he saying I was too intense? Too much of a perfectionist? Too demanding? Lately, all I heard was Casey's name as he sang her praises. "Thanks for your help in the kitchen, Casey. Casey, you have such lovely manners. I really like the way you've set out your history project, Casey. Casey, you're doing a great job with that." Casey, Casey, Casey.

To make matters worse, Mom supported him with positive comments of her own. "Chris, I could never get Casey to help before. She's a changed girl since moving in here. It's been so good for her."

Great for Casey, but what about me? Did anyone notice how I had been affected? I had always been a single child and was used to attention from both my parents. After my adopted mom passed away, Dad never hesitated to put things aside so he could spend time with me. But now everyone else came first. Mom, Casey, and Lucas; as long as they were settling in and feeling welcome, it was all that mattered. Deep down, I knew I was exaggerating, but I couldn't help my feelings.

"I'm just trying to make them welcome, Ali," Dad countered when I challenged him. "You need to be more accommodating, as well."

19

I let out a loud huff at that comment. Dad still had the luxury of a private place in his home office. Between Casey and Lucas, there was always someone at my side.

That morning was no different. "Come and play with me, Ali," Lucas insisted, tugging on my hand. He had a new play station game and wanted me to join in. But playing with Lucas was not what I felt like doing first thing on a Saturday morning.

When Casey received a phone call from Jake, it was the final straw, and I had a sudden need to escape. I didn't want to listen to her conversation with her boyfriend. Since they'd become official, they were closer than ever. *Oh yes, Jake. No, Jake. Whatever you say, Jake. That'd be so cool Jake.* I gritted my teeth at the thought.

"I'm just going out to check the mailbox," I said to Lucas, as he reached for the play station controller. "I'll be back in a few minutes."

I needed to get out of the house, even for just a few minutes, and when I stepped into the morning sunshine, I welcomed the warmth on my face. As I did so, I spotted a girl stepping off the Johnsons' front porch. I watched her walk over to their car and open the rear door.

Taking my time, I wandered down to the mailbox and pretended to search the interior, even though I knew there were no deliveries on weekends. When I turned back towards the house, I was aware of the girl looking my way, a purple canvas tote bag in her hand.

Catching her eye, I lifted my arm in a friendly wave. "Hey," I said with a smile as I continued along the pavement.

She faltered for a moment, and then a timid smile filled her features. If I didn't speak up, the opportunity would be lost.

"My name's Ali," I called out, hoping to encourage her to introduce herself as well.

"Oh, hey. I'm Alexa."

"Hi, Alexa," I replied, keeping my tone as friendly as possible. "Are you staying with the Johnsons?"

She regarded me cautiously and seemed reluctant to keep talking. But then she nodded her head. "Yeah, I am; with my brother. The Johnsons are our aunt and uncle."

My eyebrows shot up in surprise. "Oh, wow! How long are you staying for?"

"I'm not sure. For a little while, I guess."

"Oh, that's so cool. Maybe we can hang out sometime?"

She gave me a hesitant shrug. "Yeah, maybe."

At the sound of a car pulling up on the street, I turned to see Jake getting out and reaching for his bike from the trunk. Casey had obviously invited him over. Although she and I hadn't made any plans for the day, I was hoping we could do something fun together. Now that Jake had arrived, my idea of spending time alone with my twin would go by the wayside.

His visits were becoming more and more frequent, another scenario that had started to bother me. Secretly, I knew I was jealous. I wished his cousin, Mike, would show the same interest in me. We texted fairly regularly, but I didn't see him too often. If only he and I could become official too, then we could all hang out together.

Sighing, I waved at Jake as he wheeled his bike over.

"Hey, Ali. How're things?" His usual friendly smile was fixed on his face.

"Hi, Jake. I'm good, thanks." Aware that Alexa was still in her spot, I pointed in her direction. "Jake, this is Alexa. She's visiting her aunt and uncle."

"Hi, Alexa, nice to meet you," Jake said with a friendly nod of his head.

"Hi." Alexa's lips curved into a smile as her gaze lingered on Jake.

"So, Alexa," I said, bringing her eyes back to my own. "I guess we'll catch up later then."

"Okay. See ya." She gave Jake another smile before hitching her tote bag onto her shoulder and turning towards the house.

As Jake and I climbed the steps to the front door, I looked back over the fence and saw Alexa staring in our direction. I gave her a quick wave, which she returned with a wave of her own.

I'd noticed her expression when Jake arrived. I knew it was his good looks that had caught her attention. It wasn't surprising. He had the same effect on everyone.

My twin, however, was the lucky one. She was the girl he had fallen for, and when she opened the front door, and he reached for her hand, a sliver of envy erupted inside me.

CHAPTER FIVE

Alexa

At first, I wasn't sure of the girl who lived next door. She seemed friendly enough, and she was certainly very pretty. I could also tell that her family was wealthy. As well as her beautiful house, which looked even more impressive from the outside than my aunt and uncle's, her clothes were a dead give-away. Wearing a designer style jacket and the latest converse sneakers, it was obvious she shopped in the best stores. My class at school was filled with girls just like her.

They wouldn't be seen dead talking to me though. To those girls, I was an outsider, not one of the cool group and a girl they shied away from. But I'd stopped allowing them to intimidate me. I had learned long ago to stand up for myself, and as I grew older, my confidence in that department had grown as well.

I'd learned to be suspicious, and I had also learned not to let my guard down. That way, I could figure out who and what I was dealing with, as well as how to act so I could benefit in some way. I called it survival. Inside, I was marshmallow, soft and mushy. But my exterior was as tough as nails, and those snooty girls soon learned not to mess with me.

Kids like Ali couldn't be trusted. They'd pretend to be friendly and then, just as quickly, stab me in the back with their mean comments and mean looks. I was never good enough. But I'd learned to stand up for myself, and I didn't take that sort of behavior from anyone anymore. In fact, I encouraged the challenge.

Regardless of Ali's friendly manner, I made sure to

keep a protective barrier in place. I'd been caught out by letting my guard down before, and it only ended in humiliation. I didn't want that to happen again. My aunt and uncle were wealthy, so she probably assumed I came from a rich family too. If so, she definitely hadn't taken my shabby clothes into account. Either that or she pretended not to notice.

As I reached the steps leading to the front porch, I took a quick look back at the boy who had just turned up with his bike. Jake, she said his name was. He must be her boyfriend. So typical. Girls like Ali always managed to get the good looking boys. I heaved out a sigh as I stepped inside. I had plenty of other things to be worrying about, and the discovery of a good looking boy wasn't one of them.

I returned to the kitchen where my brother was finishing off a second helping of scrambled eggs piled onto freshly toasted bread smeared with butter. Uncle Vern's cooking was delicious; it was the tastiest breakfast Tyler and I had eaten in a long time and certainly beat the bowl of cheap no-frills cereal we normally scoffed down every morning.

My aunt appeared in the doorway, and her brow creased at the sight of the grubby tote bag on my shoulder. "I'll show you to your rooms," she said beckoning for Tyler and me to follow her up the stairs. "I've taken the liberty of buying a few clothes for each of you. I had to guess the sizing, but the store assistant helped me with some styles. There are a few to choose from. If there is anything that doesn't fit, leave the tags attached, and I'll take it back. But I'd prefer if you changed straight away. I can't have you roaming the neighborhood dressed like that." She cast a downward glance at each of us. "What would the neighbors think?"

I shot her a cautious look. Little did she know, I'd already met the neighbor, and she had even invited me to hang out. But I didn't dare mention that fact to Aunt Beth.

She was already stressed, and we needed to avoid upsetting her further, or she'd be likely to toss Tyler and me out on the street.

We both needed to be on our best behavior, so we could stay where we were for as long as possible.

I was a good actor, though, and I was capable of laying on the good girl charm if I needed to. My mom had often said I had a split personality and reminded everyone in the trailer park to watch out for her evil daughter. "Don't get on her bad side," she often joked.

After years of fending for myself, I had learned how to act according to the situation at hand. And this was one situation where some good acting skills would benefit Tyler and me. I just had to make sure my brother realized that as well and remind him to keep his angry outbursts in check.

He gave me an uneasy look. In addition to Aunt Beth's stern manner, the new surroundings were making him nervous. He was clearly out of his comfort zone.

Don't worry, Tyler, I thought to myself. *I feel exactly the same way.*

At least our uncle had been friendly during the drive from the trailer park. His personality was very different from his wife's. She was unfriendly and abrupt, whereas Uncle Vern was chatty and nice. They were different in every way imaginable.

But regardless of how welcoming Uncle Vern was, Aunt Beth was adamant when she spoke to Mom on the phone. "This is only a temporary arrangement!"

But what did that mean? Would she allow us to stay until our mom got her life sorted out? Or would we be sent off to foster care as soon as a random family became available?

Surely we were better off staying with relatives than being tossed into the foster system that I'd heard so many terrible things about?

Deciding that Tyler and I needed to make as good an impression as possible, I hurried along behind my aunt, wondering what my room would look like and if she had bought any clothes that I'd be remotely interested in wearing.

As soon as Aunt Beth left my bedroom, I closed the door and did a flying leap onto the bed, reveling in how comfortable it was. My bed in the trailer had consisted of a lumpy second-hand mattress that sagged in the middle. In comparison, this bed felt like a cloud beneath me, and with the soft blue comforter that covered the top, as well as the array of decorative cushions, the bed was a gift from heaven.

On the walls hung a couple of modern paintings that helped to brighten the space, but I imagined covering the walls in posters of my choosing. I had often stared in envy at the bedrooms of my friends. Their walls were filled with posters of famous pop singers and actors as well as a variety of cute ornaments, pretty photo frames, and other assortments adorning the shelves.

I had always dreamed of having my own bedroom one day. The *'bedroom'* of the trailer had a section at the end where Tyler, my mom, and I all slept. It was separated from the main area by a flimsy curtain that did nothing to keep out the blaring noise of the TV. After that, a room to myself was a dream come true.

Opening the closet where my aunt said she'd stored some clothes, I was met with yet another huge surprise. Neatly stacked on the shelves, was a selection of colorful items that beckoned me to try them on. Pulling them out, one at a time, I let out a soft squeal as I held them against me. Were these all for me? Were they mine to keep? My head spun with delight as I took everything in.

Startled by the sound of the bedroom door being pushed open, I jumped guiltily. As far as I knew, I wasn't doing anything wrong, but my aunt had me on edge, and I couldn't help my reaction. When I saw my brother's face, his mouth split into a wide grin as he held his arms out and indicated the new outfit he was wearing, I was able to breathe again.

I beamed at him. "Wow! Tyler, you look so handsome in that sweater! The color suits you so much. And I love your jeans!"

I nodded in admiration, and his smile widened even further. Like me, he was thrilled about the surprising gifts from our aunt. Although her main aim was to avoid being embarrassed by the shabby clothes her niece and nephew had arrived in, I didn't care. And neither did my brother. If she wanted to shower us with new outfits, we would happily accept.

"Here, let me pull the price tag off." I reached for the strip of cardboard that sat on his shoulder and carefully pulled it free.

When I saw the price, I blew out a surprised gasp and

quickly checked the tag on the black skinny jeans he was wearing, only to find that the figure was even higher. Aunt Beth certainly hadn't skimped on her choices. If all our clothes were in a similar price range, then it would certainly add up to a considerable sum, probably enough to pay our rent in the trailer for a month and feed us as well. The irony wasn't lost on me. Although, if Aunt Beth did help my mom financially, she would have gambled it away, which was probably why she didn't offer.

"Why don't you go and show Aunt Beth," I suggested tactfully, hoping Tyler would head downstairs and give me a chance to enjoy my selection of clothing. I noticed his reluctance and nodded encouragingly. "Just be extra polite, and I'm sure she'll be nice to you. You look so neat and tidy. She won't be able to resist you."

He heaved out an anxious breath, and my heart melted for my brother. "How about you go and find Uncle Vern? Maybe he'll get your skateboard out of the car and let you ride it in the driveway. Just remember your manners."

Our uncle was a much safer option, and Tyler's mouth curved into a semblance of a smile as he turned and headed out of the room. I closed the door behind him and picked up a pretty purple skirt that flared out at the hem, deciding to team it with a pale pink top that was covered in dark pink love hearts. Taking a quick glance at the price tag as I pulled each item on, I huffed at the numbers staring back at me. Even though the quality of the fabric was soft against my skin, the ridiculous prices were beyond belief for a kid like me.

I looked in the full-length mirror on the closet door and nodded in approval. Whoever had assisted Aunt Beth with her choices had done a wonderful job. I loved absolutely everything she had bought. I did a twirl and smiled as the skirt spun out around me. Accustomed to the hand-me-downs passed on from a friend of my mother, who had a daughter a few years older than me, the brand new clothing made me feel like a different person entirely. Instead of being embarrassed by the moth-eaten sweaters and scruffy pants that I was used to wearing, I'd be able to hold my head up and look people in the eye.

As the weather was cold outside, I decided the pair of blue jeans might be a better option. Choosing a silky soft, long-sleeved t-shirt, I tugged it carefully over my head and matched it with the white sneakers that I found at the bottom of the closet. They were a little big for my feet, but I didn't care. Picking up a patterned clutch purse that happened to be sitting on an upper shelf, I unzipped it and looked inside. The interior was empty. I wasn't sure if it was meant for me or if it was one of Aunt Beth's, but I held it against my side and looked at my reflection. It was a cool look and one I couldn't wait to show my friends when I went back to school.

They wouldn't recognize me, and I grinned at the thought.

I could certainly get used to the new clothes as well as the lovely bedroom I'd been given. Could my brother and I convince Aunt Beth to let us stay? As I twirled once more in front of the mirror, I imagined the possibility.

All of a sudden, an unwelcome vision of Aunt Beth's stern features came to mind, and it was like a slap in the face, forcing me to take a reality check. The room and the clothes were all an illusion that could be whipped away in an instant.

I'd learned a long time ago not to raise my hopes because that always led to disappointment. Gut-wrenching, shattering disappointment was something that had happened time and time again over the years. It was something I still struggled to deal with.

I had my younger brother to think of. He had been through too much already, and I needed to prepare him, just in case.

It was the only way to cope because, without warning, things could suddenly become a whole lot worse.

CHAPTER SIX

Casey

The weather was perfect for bike riding, and I had the urge to grab Jake's arm and get going. Anything to avoid the looks that Ali kept shooting my way. What was her problem anyway? I hadn't planned for Jake to come over; his phone call was totally unexpected. If only Mike could have come along too. The problem was, Mike lived a long way away. Unless he stayed over at Jake's on weekends, Ali didn't see him very much. I knew that bothered my sister, especially because I spent so much time with Jake. But that wasn't my fault, so I reminded myself not to feel guilty.

Admittedly though, if I were in Ali's shoes, I'd feel the same way.

"Do you want to come for a ride with us, Ali?" I asked in a half-hearted effort to include her.

"No, thanks. I have an essay to write. You know, the English one that's due on Monday?"

I knew exactly what she was hinting at… rather than a long bike ride, I should be completing my school work, in particular, the essay I hadn't even started yet. Ali, on the other hand, had almost finished hers. I stifled an eye roll. If she wanted to be a book nerd, that was her choice. I had invited her to come along with Jake and me, what more could I do?

Ignoring her comment, I pulled on Jake's arm. Leaving Ali behind would give me a chance to be alone with him, something I was looking forward to. As well, I wanted to meet the girl next door. Ali said she wasn't very friendly, but maybe she was shy. A new girl in the neighborhood could be fun, even if she only stayed for a short while.

I retrieved my bike from the garage and wheeled it onto the lawn where Lucas and the boy I had seen from my bedroom window, were riding skateboards along our driveway. Mom had bought Lucas a skateboard for Christmas, hoping it would encourage him away from the play station and give him something to do outdoors. But the skateboard had barely been touched. However, as soon as he looked out the window and saw the boy next door using his skateboard, it was all the encouragement my brother needed.

The other kid was a very good skateboarder, and I watched him speed down the driveway, where he made a sharp turn just before hitting the road.

Lucas turned to me and grinned. "His name's Tyler. He's been giving me some tips. Watch this!" Lucas stepped onto his skateboard and went flying along the drive.

"Careful, Lucas. Watch out for cars!" I called out loudly.

Lucas ignored me and turned onto the street where he fell off his skateboard and onto the road.

I hurried over to him. "Are you okay?"

"Yeah, I'm fine," he mumbled, dusting gravel from the knees of his jeans and darting an embarrassed glance at Tyler.

"Maybe you should wear your knee pads, and the elbow ones too. Plus, your helmet?" I added.

Lucas shook his head, obviously trying to impress the other kid. "Nah, I don't need them."

I looked at Tyler. "Hey, Tyler. Welcome to the neighborhood."

"Hey." Tyler gave me a brief nod before riding his board back up the driveway. He then sped down, this time at breakneck speed and spinning the board to a halt in front of us.

"That was so cool!" Lucas exclaimed. "Show my sister how you can do a fakie."

"What's a fakie?" I laughed.

Jake explained while Tyler demonstrated the trick, twisting and turning and lifting the skateboard into the air.

"That's awesome," Jake said, smiling with approval.

"I used to have a really good skateboard, and I could do way better fakies. But it got stolen," Tyler huffed, slamming his right fist into his left hand.

Raising my eyebrows, I decided to change the subject. "You were with a girl this morning. Is that your sister?"

"Yeah, Alexa."

"Maybe I can meet her sometime."

"You already met her. I saw you talking to her from the kitchen window."

Before I had a chance to explain that my twin had been speaking to Alexa and not me, Tyler skated to the top of the driveway and flew back down.

"Careful, Tyler!" I yelled.

Ignoring my warning, he sped out onto the street, narrowly missing a passing car.

"Maybe you guys could hang out in the backyard or even inside?" I suggested to Lucas. While it was great to see my brother using his skateboard, Tyler's skills were way too advanced for him. Lucas was sure to get hurt.

"Wanna go inside, Tyler?" Lucas called out to his new friend. "I've got some cool play station games."

"Okay. I'll just go and check with my aunt. I'll be back in a minute."

When Tyler took off, I turned to Lucas. "Maybe you should check with Mom as well."

Without hesitating, Lucas ran inside. Tyler was older and more reckless, but he would keep Lucas occupied and out of Ali's way. Mom just needed to be warned.

Swinging my leg over my bike, I pedaled along the

pavement with Jake alongside me. There was a bike track that began at the end of the street, and it followed the path of a winding creek. Jake and I had ridden along the track before, and we were both familiar with it. As we rode, I pushed thoughts of the new neighbors aside and focused on Jake instead.

With his regular football training sessions and all my commitments, we rarely had time to hang out together at school. Because of this, our weekend catch-ups were even more special, and I was thrilled to be spending time with him. Ali sometimes complained about his visits. They didn't happen very often, but my sister thought otherwise.

Since becoming an official 'couple,' Jake had also become one of my best friends. Of course, Brie had been my best friend forever, and that would never change. And Ali was more than a sister. She was my best friend, too. But my relationship with Jake had taken on a whole new meaning. We connected in a way that was different from my friendship with the girls. I could talk about my problems with Jake, and he always understood. We never argued or disagreed about anything.

With a brother of his own, he knew all about sibling rivalry, something I had always dealt with daily because of Lucas. But the recent issues with Ali were new for me, ones I had never expected to happen with my twin. Not when we were originally so excited to become a real family.

"Maybe you should try talking things through," Jake suggested when we stopped for a rest. "If you tell her how you feel, she'll probably understand."

I gave him a reluctant nod. "Yeah, I guess you're right."

"You guys have had problems before, but you've always sorted them out," he reminded me.

I'd confided in Jake about pretty much everything that had happened between my twin and me in the past. He was aware of the issues we'd faced. I knew communicating with Ali would help, as long as she was prepared to listen to my side of the argument.

Somehow, I needed to set things right, so I decided to take a leap and accept Jake's advice. It was the best alternative. It had worked on previous occasions and was something I really should try again.

We sat down on a grassy slope to enjoy the warm sunshine and the rush of the flowing creek in front of us. Jake reached for my hand, and as his fingers entwined with mine, a shiver of happiness ran down my spine, washing away all my concerns about my twin.

With Jake in my life, I could tackle anything.

CHAPTER SEVEN

Ali

I heard loud shrieks from Lucas and the boy from next door as the sound of laser fire blasted out from the play station. Mom kept asking them to keep the noise down, but it was to no avail. Dad was trying to work in his office down the hall from the TV room. If I could hear the commotion from my room upstairs, it would surely be bothering him as well.

He was very tolerant of Lucas, a fact I couldn't understand. Didn't the boisterous behavior annoy him? Or was it only me? I sighed in frustration. Before moving in with us, Lucas had always been rowdy but nothing like the kid he had become.

"It's all for attention," Mom kept reminding me. "Just ignore him, and he'll settle down."

Well, it wasn't that easy because Lucas had given up on our mom and had turned to me for attention. It was because Mom and Dad were so wrapped up in each other and were oblivious to everything going on around them.

This included the rowdiness from my nine-year-old brother. Grandma Ann was the only one who could keep him in line, and I almost wished she lived with us so she could control him. Almost. Grandma Ann's strict rules had quickly worn very thin, and I reminded myself of how things had been while our parents were on honeymoon. My dad and I had always had an easy routine, and there was never a need for many rules. Grandma Ann had a different opinion.

At least that morning, Lucas was occupied with his new friend, which gave me a chance to complete my school work.

After a while, I headed downstairs for a snack, passing by the TV room to check on the two boys. Tyler was older than Lucas, but they seemed to be getting along well, so much so that Lucas hadn't felt the need to bother me at all.

At the sound of a knock on the front door, I walked into the foyer to open it, wondering if Casey and Jake had returned. Instead, I was surprised to see Alexa standing on the doormat.

"Alexa, hi," I said, opening the door wider and wondering if she wanted to take up my invitation to hang out.

She gave me a hesitant smile. "Hey, um, my aunt sent me over to get Tyler."

"Oh, sure. Come on in. He's in the TV room with my brother. They're playing a new play station game. They've been hooked on it for the last couple of hours."

Squeals from the two boys rang out as I led Alexa through the house. "It's good for Lucas to have a playmate. Stops him from annoying me," I chuckled.

I turned around, expecting to see Alexa right behind me, but she had only taken a few steps. Her attention was focused on the interior of the house as she gazed around her. When she realized I was watching, a pink blush formed on her cheeks, and she quickened her pace.

"He's just in here," I said, pointing in the direction of the TV room.

She stood in the doorway and regarded her brother, whose eyes were glued to the TV screen. "Tyler, come on, we have to go. Aunt Beth has lunch ready."

"Aww, not yet," Tyler moaned. "I'm in the middle of a game."

"You need to come now. We can't keep her waiting." Alexa shot me an awkward look before urging her brother again. "Come on, Tyler."

Ignoring her, he continued to press on the controller and shoot out more laser beams as his gaming character ran for cover.

"Can't he stay a bit longer?" Lucas pleaded. "He can have lunch with us, can't he, Ali?"

"Tyler's welcome to stay, but I think his aunt wants him to go home. Maybe he can come back later?" I looked questioningly at Alexa.

"Maybe." She shrugged. "See what our aunt says. We just arrived today, so..." She left her sentence unfinished, and I could see she was eager to leave.

"Sure, I understand. But any time you guys want to come over, you're more than welcome."

"Okay, thanks."

I was doing my best to encourage her, but it didn't seem to be working.

"Come on, Tyler," she urged her brother once more.

Finally, he stood up from his seat. "I'll see ya later, Lucas."

"Okay," Lucas replied. "Come back after lunch if you can."

"Alright, I will." He gave me a passing smile as he followed his sister.

Just as he and Alexa reached the open doorway, Casey and Jake walked up onto the porch. I saw Alexa and her brother do a double-take, looking from Casey to me and back again. Their reaction was the same look of surprise my twin and I had seen endless times before.

"You two look exactly the same!" Tyler exclaimed.

"We're twins," Casey laughed. "My name's Casey."

"So," Tyler added, taking in Casey's clothing and processing the scene. "You were outside when I was skateboarding with Lucas?"

"Yeah," Casey answered with a nod.

"But I thought that was you," Tyler said, looking at me and shaking his head. "Identical twins, that's so cool."

Alexa's eyes were still darting between Casey and me. "How do people tell you apart?"

I smiled at her. "Usually, I braid my hair. But it's the weekend, and I couldn't be bothered."

"Oh." Alexa's smile lit up her features.

Maybe she was shy, or a little reserved, or perhaps she just needed some time to get to know us. If Lucas was going to hang out with Tyler, and Casey was occupied with Jake, perhaps I could get to know Alexa a little better.

If she would let me.

I was about to say something more when Mom appeared beside us. She gave Alexa a warm smile. "Hi there. Are you Tyler's sister?"

Alexa nodded. "Yeah, I'm Alexa."

"Lovely to meet you, Alexa. Are you guys on vacation?"

"Um, not really. Our mom's been sick, so our aunt and uncle are looking after us for a while."

I looked at Alexa and frowned. Her mother must be very ill. I thought of my adopted mother and hoped Alex's mom wasn't suffering anything too serious.

"I'm sorry to hear that," Mom said, not pushing any further. "I hope your mother is okay. If you're ever looking for something to do and the girls aren't busy, you're welcome to come over. You too, Tyler. Lucas has really enjoyed your company this morning."

"Yes!" Lucas squealed. "Come over whenever you want, Tyler."

"You're welcome anytime as well, Alexa," I added encouragingly.

Casey nodded. "Yeah, it'd be fun to hang out sometime."

"Maybe you could all come for dinner?" Mom said, not skipping a beat. "I've been planning to invite your aunt and uncle for a while now."

Alexa gave her a hesitant nod.

"What about tomorrow night?" Mom pressed, looking at Ali and me.

I nodded eagerly. "That'd be fun."

Mom turned back to Alexa. "I'll pop over a bit later and check with your aunt and uncle."

"Awesome!" Lucas yelped happily and gave Tyler a quick high-five.

There were very few kids in our neighborhood, and apart from an occasional visit from his best friend, Matt, who also happened to be Jake's younger brother, there was no one for Lucas to play with.

Alexa nudged Tyler. "We'd better get going. Um, nice to meet you, Mrs…"

"Jackson," Mom said.

"Bye, Mrs. Jackson. Thanks for having Tyler over." Alexa gave us a quick wave and led her brother out the door.

I watched them walk along the pavement and turn into their yard. Alexa took another look back at me. I waved again, and this time, Alexa's response seemed more enthusiastic. I even caught the remnants of a smile on her face.

Perhaps we could become friends, after all.

CHAPTER EIGHT

Alexa

When I saw that the two girls had the same face and hair, it was kind of freaky. Except for their clothes, there was no way to tell them apart. I had never met a pair of identical twins before, but I noticed they dressed quite differently and seemed to have different personalities as well. While first impressions were sometimes misleading, I was usually a good judge of character from the very beginning.

Casey was the more casual and laid back twin. It was obvious in the way she dressed. But then, she'd just gone for a bike ride. I knew that because I'd caught a glimpse of her and her boyfriend from my bedroom window. At the time, I thought she was Ali and that she'd changed into different clothes. Now I knew otherwise.

So, Jake was Casey's boyfriend and not Ali's. I wondered how Ali felt about that. If I had a sister with a boyfriend who looked like him, I'd be totally jealous. It made me curious as to why he had chosen Casey and not her twin. It was a detail I'd like to learn more about.

I hadn't expected to make any friends, especially in such a wealthy neighborhood. But Ali seemed keen to get to know me, which was a novelty I wasn't used to from a girl like her.

In the past, keeping my guard up had become my defense mechanism, my way of protecting myself. I'd been shut down and trodden on so often by kids who thought they were better than me, and I didn't want to let it happen again. By staying aloof, I could keep the haters at bay. It was like a shield to ward off the mixture of pity and mean bullying.

Maybe Ali was one of the rare ones, though? I really wasn't sure.

My mind raced as I walked with Tyler back to our aunt's house. He was busy chattering alongside me, but I barely registered a word. Ali wasn't the type I tended to gravitate to, but she was more outgoing and welcoming than her sister. Casey was wrapped up in Jake and probably didn't have time for anyone else.

My thoughts then wandered to the interior of their house. My aunt and uncle's place was impressive, but the Jackson's house was even nicer, and I couldn't help staring when I entered the foyer. With the wide staircase flowing from the upper level, it was like a scene from a movie where a girl dressed in a beautiful gown stepped gracefully down to the lower floor. I imagined myself in that scene when I was older.

As if that would ever happen to me. I rolled my eyes at the idea — what a joke.

I recalled the questioning look on Ali's face when she caught me staring, and my skin prickled with heat. I was so in awe, so out of my comfort zone, it was embarrassing. I just wanted to grab Tyler and leave.

Meanwhile, I wondered what my aunt and uncle would have to say about the dinner invitation. Aunt Beth wasn't the friendliest of people, but maybe she was different when dealing with the neighbors. I guessed that only time would tell.

Before I had a chance to mention Mrs. Jackson's offer, our aunt ushered us into the bathroom to wash our hands before eating. As soon as we sat down at the kitchen table, she let out a bombshell, which caused me to stare at her open-mouthed. The revelation was something that neither Tyler nor I had anticipated at all.

Her eyes roamed between my brother and me as she

spoke. "While you're staying with us, you'll both attend the local school. I've done some research, and the school bus stops just down the street. Apparently, that school has a very good reputation."

I sat in my spot aghast, and the knot in my stomach returned. I hadn't considered the fact that our school was nearly an hour's drive in a car. If we took the bus, there'd probably be several connections, and it would take us forever to get there.

Aunt Beth's expression softened just a little. "With any luck, the children next door might be enrolled at the same school. Then you'll know someone."

"Yeah, but Lucas is younger than me," Tyler scoffed. "He wouldn't be in my class. Why can't we go to our old school?"

"That's out of the question," Aunt Beth snapped, the glimmer of softness whipping away. "How do you think you'd get there? Your uncle and I both leave early for work. We can't drive you, and it's too far to attempt public transport."

"I don't want to go to a new school," Tyler grumbled.

"While you're in this house, you'll do as you're told." At the sound of Aunt Beth's no-nonsense tone, Tyler clamped his lips together.

He gave me a black look, and I nudged him with my foot under the table. *Please behave, Tyler,* I begged him silently. *She'll kick us out if you don't.*

"We've heard great things about that school," Uncle Vern offered gently. "I'm sure you'll make new friends quickly."

Tyler poked angrily at his toasted sandwich, causing the melted cheese to ooze out the sides. I nudged him with my shoe again. Thankfully, it was enough to get my message across, and instead of a rude retort, he picked up the sandwich and bit into it.

I chewed silently, all the while thinking about the

kids who lived next door. As Aunt Beth had said, if they went to the same school, it would make things a lot easier. But even though the twins seemed friendly, girls like them would never want to be seen at school with the likes of me. Hanging out on weekends when no one else was around was one thing, but they'd never invite me into their group at school.

During the remainder of lunch, Uncle Vern chatted on, and I knew he was trying to ease the tension in the room. I was grateful for his efforts and answered as politely as I could. In contrast, Aunt Beth's cool manner remained fixed in place.

After lunch, she insisted that Tyler and I remain at home. "You've only just arrived. I don't want you annoying our neighbors anymore today."

I was content to take advantage of the massive TV screen in the media room and the chance to watch some Netflix shows I'd heard about. The idea of a *media room* was so cool, especially with a pair of super comfy reclining couches in place. Such luxuries were unfamiliar to Tyler and me, and I was ready to enjoy them. Plus, staying out of our aunt's way was a good option.

Later that afternoon, as I was leaving the bathroom, there was a knock at the front door. Aunt Beth pulled it open, and I saw Mrs. Jackson's smiling face as I made my way along the hallway. A friendly smile formed on my aunt's face as well. It was one I didn't know she was capable of.

"Jackie, hello. How are you?" she asked in a welcoming tone.

Shuffling into an adjoining room, I peeked out from behind the door, so I could watch the scene unnoticed. What interested me most was my aunt's manner. It was the opposite of what I was used to.

"I'm really well, thanks," the twins' mother replied.

"I hope Tyler wasn't a nuisance earlier," Aunt Beth

chuckled. "I know what boys are like. They can be so rowdy."

I frowned at her remark. What did she know about kids? She'd never had any of her own, and she'd had nothing to do with Tyler and me until now.

"No, not at all," Mrs. Jackson countered. "Lucas really enjoyed Tyler's company, and it was lovely to meet Alexa too."

I stepped back further into the shadows, ensuring I couldn't be seen. It would be embarrassing to be caught out.

"Actually, the reason for my visit," Jackie continued, "is to invite you for dinner tomorrow evening. We'd love to have you over. My kids would like to spend some time with your niece and nephew, as well."

"Oh, Jackie, that's so sweet of you, but I'd hate to impose."

"Don't be silly," Jackie laughed. "Chris and I have wanted to invite you for a while now. So what do you say? Will tomorrow night work?"

Aunt Beth had no option, and I smirked. She was

used to being the one in control.

"As long as you're sure it's no trouble, we'd love to come."

I rolled my eyes at her response. I had only spent a few hours with my aunt, but I could already tell when she was faking.

"What can I bring?" she added.

"Just yourselves," Mrs. Jackson replied. "Shall we say five-thirty? With school on Monday, it's probably best to have an early start."

"Five thirty sounds great," Aunt Beth said. "I'm looking forward to it already."

I choked back another smirk and tip-toed down the hallway to the media room so I could share the news with Tyler. The invitation would help to cheer him up. His mouth curved into a pleased smile, but it didn't hide the sadness lurking in his eyes. As well as facing a new school, we had a mother who didn't want us, a fact that Tyler was well aware of. He wasn't stupid; he understood the situation as well as the uncertainty our future held. We were forced out of our dumpy old trailer, but it was the place we had called home for as long as we could remember. There, we had some security, and our mom was our mom, after all.

I was much more resilient than my younger brother. He was only eleven years old and needed a parent in his life. Even if ours was a woman addicted to gambling, Tyler was just a kid, and having our mother in his life was better than no mother at all.

Her face flitted through my thoughts, and I wondered if she was thinking of us. Did she feel guilty? Would she miss us and try to improve her situation so we could be together again? Or would she simply continue her bad habits?

I wasn't at all hopeful about her finding a job and a decent place to live. I knew her too well; Tyler and I were a burden she could do without. The pipe-dream of us being a happy family with a secure and stable home life was one that would more than likely never eventuate.

We now had new circumstances to deal with. So far, I didn't think our uncle minded having us around. Would it be possible to convince Aunt Beth to feel the same way and allow us to stay long term?

Or was that another ridiculous pipe-dream, one that I shouldn't even consider?

CHAPTER NINE

Alexa

Our first night went by without too much of a hitch. We all ate dinner together, a delicious chicken casserole cooked by our uncle. Tyler and I weren't used to such delicious home-cooked meals. I'd lost count of the times we had eaten dry cereal or two-minute noodles for dinner back in our trailer.

When Uncle Vern placed a steaming hot apple pie on the table for dessert, I thought Tyler's eyes would pop out of his head.

Served with vanilla ice cream, it was a taste sensation, and my brother and I both accepted a second helping. When I saw Aunt Beth's brow creased into a frown, I wondered if we had done the wrong thing. Perhaps she was planning leftovers for the following day. I knew food was expensive but didn't they have plenty of money?

I ate the remainder of my meal in silence and was glad when our aunt left the table, saying she had work to complete in her office. Tyler and I helped Uncle Vern to tidy the kitchen, and then we joined him in the media room where we watched a comedy on TV. Whenever Aunt Beth wasn't around, the atmosphere was relaxed and easy. Before long, each of us was in fits of laughter over the pranks of the actors. It allowed my brother and me to switch off for a while and forget about the uncertainty hanging over our heads.

When I later noticed Tyler falling asleep on the couch beside me, I nudged him awake and led him up the stairs to his room. He had showered earlier and had changed into an old pair of track pants and a t-shirt. They were worn out and scruffy, but at least they were clean. Aunt Beth grimaced when she saw them, of course, and said she would put pajamas on the list of supplies she planned to purchase the following day. But at bedtime, our aunt was nowhere to be seen, and for that I was glad.

Tyler climbed sleepily into bed, and I pulled the comforter up to his chin.
He snuggled under the cozy thickness, and as I tucked it around him, his eyes locked on mine. "Alexa?"

"Yes, Tyler?"

"What's going to happen to us?"

"What do you mean?" I asked, even though I knew very well what he was referring to.

"If Aunt Beth doesn't let us stay here, where will we go?"

I sucked in a breath and steeled myself to answer. Tears threatened at the corners of my eyes, and it was an effort to hold them back. I couldn't let Tyler see me cry.

"Let's not think about that for now. We're very lucky to be here; we should just focus on that."

He let out a worried breath. "But what if Aunt Beth makes us leave?"

I paused before answering. I wouldn't make a promise that I couldn't keep. Our future was more uncertain than it had ever been, and Tyler needed to be prepared. But I struggled for something to say.

"Whatever happens, Tyler, we've got each other, okay?" I said, gently brushing the hair from his eyes. "I'm your big sister, and I'll look after you. So you have nothing to worry about."

"Promise?"

"Cross my heart." Blinking the tears away, I crossed my finger over my chest then leaned down to kiss his forehead. "Now go to sleep, and I'll see you in the morning."

I got to my feet before the tears had a chance to spill out. Moving to the doorway, I flicked off the overhead light. "I'll leave the door open a bit and remember, I'm right next door. If you wake up and want to jump in bed with me, that's fine. Okay?"

Tyler nodded his head and closed his eyes. A few seconds later, I could hear the steady sound of his breathing. It had been a stressful day for each of us, and I was ready for bed as well. I pulled the door partly closed and went to the bathroom where I stared at my face in the mirror.

What if Tyler was right? What if Aunt Beth insisted that we go into foster care? Would I be able to maintain my promise to my brother and keep us together? As I brushed my teeth, a whirlwind of negativity swirled around in my head.

In the house next door, were three kids who had it all. They owned all the beautiful clothes and technology and toys that money could buy, and they lived in a beautiful home. While I was envious of every one of those details, they weren't what I craved for. Those kids had parents who loved and cared for them, and that was what mattered most.

It seemed such a simple concept. Surely it was one that Tyler and I deserved as well. Was it too much to ask for? Didn't we deserve it too?

51

CHAPTER TEN

Alexa

On Sunday morning, Aunt Beth announced that she was heading to the mall to buy the extra supplies for Tyler and me. I knew she had pajamas in mind, but I wasn't sure what else.

"I can go with you?" I suggested, hoping to be able to choose my own pajamas or anything else she insisted on buying.

"No, thank you." Her quick retort made it quite clear that I wasn't welcome. "Your uncle is going to take you both to the playground. There's a very good park not far from here. You can help supervise your brother. Make sure there are no incidents."

I stifled an eye roll. Incidents? What sort of incidents was she talking about? She probably thought Tyler couldn't be trusted. Meanwhile, didn't she realize I was thirteen and had outgrown the playground a long time ago? I would much rather go shopping at the mall.

"I also need your correct shoe size," she added with a sigh. "Your sneakers are too big, aren't they?"

"I normally take a size smaller. But I'm happy to make do."

"If we're going to the Jacksons for dinner tonight, you need something dressier than sneakers!" she exclaimed.

I remembered it was all about appearances and I also wasn't going to say no to another new pair of shoes. "If I go with you, I can tell you what style I like," I offered, trying my best to be tactful.

She huffed out an impatient breath, and for a second, I thought she would agree. But then she shook her head. "I'll figure it out. Keep an eye on them, Vern," she warned her husband. "I'll be back later."

Before I could say another word, she walked through the kitchen doorway and was gone from sight.

Uncle Vern gave me a reassuring shrug and smiled. "Are you guys ready to get out of here? There are a couple of skate bowls at the park, Tyler; ideal for your skateboard."

Tyler's eyes lit up. "Cool."

"What about you, Alexa?" my uncle asked. "Are you into skateboarding too?"

Tyler burst out laughing. "Alexa's hopeless. She tried my board once and nearly broke her neck."

I rolled my eyes at him. "Skateboarding isn't my thing."

"How about we just watch Tyler together then?"

With no other option, I followed him out the front door while Tyler collected his skateboard from the garage. I climbed into the car while Uncle Vern stored the skateboard in the trunk. After a short drive, we arrived at a parking lot situated by a sprawling park that included a duck pond, a widespread playground, cycling paths, and running tracks, and the promised skate bowls. It bordered extensive bushland and was a very pretty spot. I looked forward to hanging out there on my own sometime. If Aunt Beth allowed me to, that was. It was also an ideal place to exercise. I'd joined the running team at school earlier in the semester, something I was going to miss, but the park was a great place to train so I could keep up my fitness.

I sat on a bench seat alongside my uncle where we could watch Tyler, and before long, he was calling out repeatedly.

"Did you see that, Alexa?"

"Alexa, watch this one!"

"Alexa, check this out!"

It warmed my heart to see him smiling, and I waved continually, making sure he knew I was paying attention.

Even Uncle Vern took an interest, commenting on Tyler's skills when he skated back to us. "You're an awesome skateboarder, Tyler. Very impressive!"

"Thanks!" Tyler grinned happily back.

"I used to love skateboarding when I was your age. But the only trick I ever mastered was an ollie," Uncle Vern chuckled.

"What?" Tyler laughed. "You could do an ollie?"

Uncle Vern's eyebrows shot up. "Yes, I could. You probably don't believe me, but I was pretty good at it."

"Show me," Tyler insisted, tugging on Uncle Vern's hand.

"I wish I could, but I haven't been on a skateboard in years. I'd probably end up breaking a bone."

"You couldn't be any worse than Alexa!" Tyler said, his eyes shining with amusement.

"Hey," I scoffed, giving him a playful poke with my finger.

Uncle Vern ruffled his hair. "How about some ice cream? That place over there has the biggest selection you'll ever see. And the quality is amazing."

"Yes, please!" Tyler's eyes widened at the idea of such an awesome treat.

Uncle Vern turned to me, and I gave him an enthusiastic nod. When we wandered over to the ice cream stand, he said we could choose a double scoop waffle cone if we wanted to. Tyler and I took in the array of flavors in awe. There were so many to choose from, and I thought my heart would spill over.

"Would you like to sample one?" the attendant asked with a smile. At first, I wasn't sure what she was talking about, but then she offered each of us a small spoonful of the gourmet choc chip. "This is one of our most popular."

Uncle Vern gave me a nod, and I took the spoon and popped it into my mouth. Try before you buy? It was a new experience for me, and when the attendant asked if I'd like to try another flavor as well, I could hardly believe my luck.

When I was handed a waffle cone topped with gourmet choc chip and a large scoop of honeycomb, I bit into the crunchy texture and discovered it was a taste sensation.

I gave my uncle a grateful smile. "Thank you, Uncle Vern, this is delicious."

"Yeah, thanks, Uncle Vern," Tyler piped up, his face already smeared in chocolate.

"My pleasure," Uncle Vern replied as we followed him to a nearby seat.

We sat in peaceful silence for a while, each of us content to enjoy our treat and watch the people walking by. I allowed myself to believe things really could work out for Tyler and me. Rather than focusing on all the worry and despair that I'd been so overwhelmed by, I decided to try a positive outlook instead. When Uncle Vern gave me another warm smile, my hopes soared even further.

Later that afternoon, Aunt Beth asked Tyler and me to shower and change. "Choose something from the clothes I bought you," she instructed us.

I didn't need a reminder. I'd already spent the afternoon trying on a variety of combinations, so I'd be prepared for my new school. By including a few of my own things that I hoped would pass Aunt Beth's inspection, I figured I had enough for five cool outfits, one for each day of the week. It would allow me to arrive at school, feeling happy with the way I looked.

For dinner with our neighbors, I had a special outfit in mind. The purple skinny jeans that Aunt Beth had bought fitted me to perfection, and I marveled at how lucky I was.

I also chose a matching purple shirt made of beautiful silky fabric. But my favorite addition was the coat. Olive green in color, it was lined inside with the most beautiful pink fur that extended onto the collar as well. Not only was the coat very warm, which was perfect for the lingering cold weather, it was also the prettiest coat I had ever owned. When I pulled on the new brown boots that Aunt Beth had brought home that day, I stared at them in admiration.

Of course, I would have preferred to choose some shoes, but once again, I was pleased with my aunt's selection. As well as the shoes and some new pajamas, she bought new backpacks for Tyler and me to take to school. The backpack was a pretty shade of purple. Thank goodness I loved purple. If she had bought everything in a gross color or style and forced me to wear it, it would have been the worst.

While showering, I had washed my hair, enjoying the scent of the expensive shampoo, but when Aunt Beth saw the state of my curly frizz, she looked at me in disgust.

"You look like a drowned rat!" she exclaimed. "You'll find a hairdryer in the bathroom cupboard. Please use it."

I also found a styling brush, which I used to smooth out the curls. I'd seen an ad on TV once for a similar style of

56

brush and was amazed at the result. I never thought I'd get the chance to trial the same method myself.

With my hair hanging in sleek waves over my shoulders and wearing such cool clothing, I actually felt good about myself. Picking up the backpack, I hung it on my arm and checked out my reflection. Even if Aunt Beth was putting her needs first by choosing clothes that she found acceptable, my brother and I were the ones to benefit.

When Tyler and I made our way down the stairs, we were met by Uncle Vern, who grinned with approval. "Wow! You guys look great."

Tyler shot me a pleased look. He was just as happy as me with the choices in his closet.

"Just remember your manners tonight," Aunt Beth warned us. "And remember, no one needs to know your history. Your mother is unwell with an undiagnosed illness, so you're staying with us for now. That's all people need to be told. If word got out that I have a down-and-out, gambling-addicted sister who can't even look after her own children, my reputation would be ruined."

Uncle Vern cleared his throat. I could tell how uncomfortable he was with his wife's choice of words. He was so different from her, and I wondered if they had anything at all in common.

But our aunt didn't have to worry. She'd warned us a few times previously, and the lie had already fallen easily from my lips when I was at the Jackson's house the day before. Tyler and I didn't need reminding again.

I didn't want people knowing the truth either. It was embarrassing and humiliating. It had been bad enough when the kids at school learned we lived in an old trailer, but now our situation was even worse. As well as being evicted from the trashy trailer, our mother didn't want us. There was also a big chance we'd soon be shipped off to foster care. I was more than happy to keep those details to myself. I knew my brother was just as embarrassed about our situation, and it was no effort for him to live a lie as well.

Determined to enjoy showing off my new look, I pushed my aunt's warning aside and followed everyone out into the cold evening air. As I walked, I noticed the sound the heels of my boots made as they clicked on the pavement. I pulled my coat tighter around me and smiled. If my friends could see me, they'd be shocked. Everyone, including my mother, would be amazed at the transformation.

A sliver of nervous energy wound through me as we crossed into the neighbors' front yard, and their large house loomed in front of us. Tyler rushed ahead and pressed the doorbell. As the sound rang out, I inhaled a deep breath and tried to calm my nerves. A fraction of a second later, the door swung open, and we were met by one of the twins.

I had no idea which twin she was or what the night had in store.

As far as the events ahead were concerned, all I could do was hope for a positive outcome. Contemplating anything else was just too painful.

CHAPTER ELEVEN

Casey

I smiled at our guests and welcomed them inside. At the sound of their voices, Lucas rushed over. Of all of us, he was the most excited. "Tyler, come on, let's go in the TV room."

Tyler darted a quick look at his aunt before taking another step. He was reluctant to move without her permission. I'd already noticed he was a pretty energetic kid. She had probably warned him to behave.

Mrs. Johnson put a restraining hand on his shoulder. "Tyler, say hello to the Jacksons first. Where are your manners?"

"Hello," Tyler mumbled, glancing at each of us.

Ali, Mom, and Dad had appeared behind me. Dad shook Mr. and Mrs. Johnson's hands and then reached for Tyler's as well. "Nice to meet you, young man."

Tyler hadn't been taught to greet adults in that way and hesitated at first. With a small nudge from his aunt, he shook Dad's hand. "Nice to meet you too, Mr. Jackson."

I saw Mrs. Johnson's mouth curve just the slightest bit, and she released her grip on his shoulder. After a nod of approval from her, he scurried off with Lucas. When I returned my gaze to Alex, my eyes roamed over her outfit. She looked amazing.

"I love your coat, Alexa!" I exclaimed with an impressed gasp. "Where did you get it?"

"Um, Aunt Beth bought it for me."

"Wow! It's so nice!" Ali said in agreement as she scanned Alexa's choice of clothing.

Mom and Chris led Mr. and Mrs. Johnson towards the formal living room, where some pre-dinner snacks were already laid out on the coffee table.

Rather than following them, I turned back to Alexa. "Do you want to come up to our room? Dinner won't be ready for a little while."

She gave me a cautious nod. "Okay."

"Your jeans are so pretty!" Ali exclaimed as we headed up the stairs. "I love the color."

"Thanks," Alexa said, nodding in Ali's direction.

Alexa's entire outfit was gorgeous, and I wished I'd dressed up a little more. Compared to when she first arrived in the Johnsons' driveway the morning before, she looked like a different person. Her oversized sweater and leggings when she stepped out of her uncle's car were polar opposite to what she was now wearing. And with her hair loose, she was almost unrecognizable.

I admired the ebony sheen of the dark strands. Her hair was long and shiny, nothing like the wild curls that bounced around my face. Was her hair naturally straight, or did she use a straightener? I decided to ask her that question later. For the moment, though, Ali was bombarding her with her own questions, and I wished she would back off a little and give Alexa a chance to speak.

When we entered the bedroom, Alexa's eyes flickered to each corner, taking in every aspect of the space. "Such a cool room. I love the posters on your walls," she remarked, indicating the far wall where I had pinned my favorites.

I had brought them from my old house, where they had decorated the walls for quite some time. Some were now a little tattered and torn. Ali had suggested I get new ones, but I liked keeping something from my old life. It made that section of the room a reflection of me.

"That's Casey's side," Ali pointed out. "This is my side over here. You can sit on my bed if you like."

As usual, all of Ali's things were in perfect order. Alexa sat down but didn't comment.

"What's it like being a twin?" she asked all of a sudden, catching both Ali and me by surprise.

We shared a look, and each of us hesitated to answer. If I had been asked that question a few months earlier, the words would have spilled easily from my lips. "It's amazing! We share absolutely everything. We care about each other, we pick up on each other's feelings, and we understand each other!"

Since moving into the same house together and sharing a room, things between Ali and me had changed. I didn't dare say that aloud, but I did wonder what was going through my twin's head. What were her thoughts these days?

Ali's eyebrows arched, and I expected the worst. But I

needn't have worried because her response was all smiles and positivity. "It's like looking in a mirror every day. We not only look alike, but we also think alike. We even complete each other's sentences. It's pretty crazy, but it's also very cool."

Ali looked at me encouragingly, and I was about to add some comments of my own, but she kept talking. "We wear the same size clothes and shoes, which gives us so many more things to wear because we can share everything. Can't we, Casey?"

I looked at her and frowned. She and I both knew I was the one who benefited. She owned twice as many clothes, and it was mostly her things that we wore. Was she bothered by that? She never used to be, but maybe she'd grown tired of me always borrowing her things. Or was I overreacting and had the wrong impression entirely?

"You're so lucky," Alexa remarked. "I wish I had a sister I could share everything with."

Ali's smile didn't meet her eyes, and I suspected that I'd guessed correctly after all. "How long do you think you'll be staying with the Johnsons, Alexa?" Ali asked, changing the subject.

Alexa gave each of us an awkward look. "I'm not sure. It depends on my mom, I guess."

I was reluctant to pry, but Ali plowed on. "What's wrong with her?"

I stifled a huff as I looked at my sister. She certainly wasn't holding back.

Alexa chewed on her lip and glanced down at the carpet. "The doctors are trying to diagnose her. We have to wait and see how she is."

It was a vague answer, and I could see she wasn't willing to discuss it. I didn't blame her. It was a private matter, and she'd only just met us.

Once again, this didn't stop Ali. "I'm so sorry; it must be really hard."

Ali gave Alexa a sympathetic look. She had lost her adopted mother to cancer. She knew full well how difficult it was to have a sick parent. Thankfully, she didn't spill out our full life story. I wasn't ready to explain all of that to our new neighbor.

"So, what about school?" Ali prompted, keen to learn as much about Alexa as she could.

"My aunt enrolled us at Somerton Middle School while we're here," Alexa explained. "I was hoping we could still go to our old school, but it's on the other side of town, so it's too far away."

"Oh my gosh, what?" Ali squealed and jumped off her bed. "That's the school we go to! You and Tyler can take the bus with us. It stops just down the road. This is going to be so cool."

"We can show you around the school," I offered quickly, determined to get a word in.

"My dad used to give me a ride on his way to work," Ali interrupted. "But now we all take the bus."

"Oh." Alexa's frown showed her confusion.

"Chris is Ali's dad," I explained briefly before Ali jumped in and said too much. "He married our mom not long ago."

"Really?" This time, Alexa's eyebrows shot up.

I smiled at her. "It's a long story. We'll tell you another time." *Perhaps when we get to know you better,* I thought to myself.

"Okay." She regarded me curiously, and I knew her mind was ticking over.

Our crazy, mixed-up story could wait. Every time we attempted to explain it, the reactions were always the same… curious expressions and prodding for more information. When they learned that Ali and I had been separated at birth, their interest spiked tenfold.

I was reminded of Ronnie Miller, our biggest rival at school. Her comment was downright mean. "Didn't your mom want you, Ali?" she sneered. "Is that why she offered you up for adoption?"

Ronnie was a huge troublemaker. Although she'd settled down for a while, she had recently started targeting us again. It was usually me who bore the brunt of her mean comments, and I was shocked by her attack on Ali. It was such a nasty thing to say. I stepped in to defend my sister and told Ronnie to go away and mind her own business.

Meanwhile, Ali's face crumpled. It wasn't the truth, but it planted a seed in my twin's mind. *My mother didn't want me, so she gave me to another family.*

Mom had assured us both that she only did what she thought was best for us at the time. As a single mom, she could only manage one child, but she made sure Ali was adopted by a loving family. Fortunately for Ali, they also rich, and I used to wonder if she was the one who had lucked out.

But how would Alexa respond if she heard that news? Would she also think Ali was unwanted? A child being given away by her mother was a difficult concept to grasp.

I returned my attention to Ali, who had moved on. "Hopefully you'll be in our class, Alexa. Ms. Harris is our teacher. She's really nice, isn't she, Casey?"

"She gives us a lot of homework, though," I groaned, thinking of the English essay I had rushed through that afternoon.

Ali had taken her time, and her essay was sure to be a masterpiece. In comparison, mine was a quick throw together. If Ali hadn't reminded me about it, it would still be sitting unfinished in my school bag.

"She's just trying to prepare us for junior high next year," Ali countered. "The work is going to be a lot tougher then."

I ignored Ali's comment and pointed to a photo frame on our bookshelf. "I can't wait to introduce you to our friend, Brie. You'll be able to meet her tomorrow."

"Brie is Casey's best friend," Ali explained.

"Well, she's your friend too."

Ali shrugged. "She's closer to you."

Deep down, I knew this was true, but I wasn't sure what Ali was getting at. And why was she acting so weird in front of Alexa? I bristled with annoyance. Brie liked Ali just as much as me. Ali was aware of that. But Brie and I had been friends since kindergarten. Did Ali feel threatened by that fact?

Alexa got up from the bed to take a closer look at the photos, picking up the one of Ali and me in our flower girl gowns. "Was this from your parents' wedding? You both look so pretty."

"Yeah," Ali replied. "It was so much fun. Neither of us had ever been a flower girl before."

Alexa took in the other pics, her eyes lingering on the honeymoon image of Mom and Chris in the swimming pool. "They look so happy."

I caught a hint of sadness in her tone. She had been

ripped away from her mom, who was suffering a terrible illness. So it was understandable.

I then wondered if her dad was around. Surely he'd look after Alexa and her brother while their mom was ill? Maybe they had an unusual story, just like Ali and me.

In an effort to cheer her up, I pulled out my phone. "What's your Instagram account name? We can Follow each other."

Alexa darted an awkward glance back. "I don't have an Instagram account."

"Oh, okay," I said with a shrug. "What about your phone number then?"

A hot blush crept across Alexa's cheeks. "Um," she stammered. "My phone broke. I have to get a new one."

I frowned at her odd reaction but brushed it off. "So hard being without a phone," I sympathized. I had no idea why Alexa reacted like that. A broken phone wasn't something to be embarrassed about.

Distracted by Lucas and Tyler, who had suddenly appeared in the doorway, we turned towards them. "Dinner's ready!" Lucas announced loudly. "Mom said to come downstairs."

He stalked away with Tyler in tow, and Ali, Alexa, and I followed them down the stairs. Perhaps in time, we'd get to know Alexa better and could share each other's stories. I looked forward to making a new friend. I could see that Ali felt the same way. If only she'd give me a chance to chat with Alexa as well.

CHAPTER TWELVE

Alexa

When I climbed into bed, my head was spinning over the events of the night. I wasn't used to girls fighting for my attention, but the past few hours had been like nothing I'd ever experienced before. The twins seemed to accept me without question, so much so that they were both eager to become my friend. No one had ever fought for my attention. It was a foreign concept.

I had no doubt my clothes had been the trigger. Just as Aunt Beth had said, appearances were everything. Because I was wearing cool clothes, the girls wanted to include me. If I'd rocked up wearing the shabby old things I usually wore, what would they think of me then?

Without a doubt, their opinions would be entirely different, especially if they learned of my circumstances. Tyler and I wouldn't be invited to hang out again, and we'd become outcasts at school; unless they saw us as a charity case, as so many people often did.

When Casey asked for my cell number, my stomach dropped. Luckily I thought of an excuse to explain why I didn't have one. I knew a few kids who weren't allowed social media accounts, so the fact that I didn't use Instagram wasn't such a big deal. But how many thirteen-year-olds didn't own a phone? At my old school, I was the only kid in my class without one. My mother could barely afford to pay for her own phone. Even though hers was an old second-hand model with a cracked screen, her monthly bill was an expense that was always overdue. Another phone was out of the question.

While at the twins' house, I'd been careful not to give away too much. It was interesting to see how rich kids lived though, and I took in every single detail of their house. The expensive furniture and décor, as well as the stylish layout, were too special for words.

When I considered the rivalry between the girls, I wondered what it was really like to be a twin. Did they always feel the need to compete? While they dressed differently, were they still seen as a reflection of each other? I noticed a lot of their belongings were the same. They owned matching phones with matching cases; the only difference was the color. Ali's was pink, and Casey's was electric blue. Even their backpacks, which sat on the floor by their desks, were identical, except for the color. Were they always given matching belongings? If I had a choice, I'd much prefer my own style, rather than having a replica of my sister's. They were individuals, after all.

Regardless of their identical looks, they had varied personalities. I'd noticed it the day before, and it was this factor that set them apart. Ali was chattier, more confident and more outgoing, and she was constantly seeking my attention. At one point, I felt sorry for Casey who was trying her hardest to be included.

If they were always together, it would be hard to be noticed unless one tried to dominate the other. Clearly, Ali had mastered that. Maybe she felt the need to. Somehow, I thought Casey was prettier, and according to Ali, Brie was Casey's best friend. Did Ali have a best friend too? Or did she share Brie with her twin, as Casey claimed? Casey also had a very cute boyfriend. I wondered if Ali had one as well. Was Ali intimidated by Casey, and this urged her to compete?

All the little details fascinated me, and I reflected on every second that had passed. According to Uncle Vern when I questioned him afterward, the house had originally belonged to Ali and her adopted parents. But then her adopted mom died of cancer, and it was just Ali and her dad. After a while, Casey's family came along, and everything changed.

I was sad to hear about her adopted mom. Losing her to cancer must have been horrible. But now she lived with her birth mom. The concept was hard to comprehend, and I was looking forward to hearing the full story. I hadn't prodded the twins for more information. That would push them to question me, something I wanted to avoid.

At least Aunt Beth was pleased with how the evening had gone. Thankfully, Tyler remembered his manners and was well-behaved. Even I was proud of him. When Mrs. Jackson commented on what lovely children we were, I caught a hint of pride in our aunt's expression.

From the moment she set foot in the Jackson home, she had taken on a new persona… chatty and friendly and funny, and likable. I even took a liking to her. But it didn't last long. As soon as the night was over, reality came crashing down.

"Straight to bed, you two!" she snapped as soon as we returned home. "You need to be ready for the bus in the morning. Vern and I will be leaving for work at the same time, and we don't want you holding us up!"

Why was she suddenly so mean and cranky? Was her earlier persona just for show? Was it simply an act to impress the neighbors? My other question was, how did Uncle Vern put up with her?

Desperate to escape her threatening look, I mumbled a quick goodnight and hurried up the stairs with Tyler shuffling along behind me. After tucking him into bed, I changed into my new pajamas. I then pulled my old ones out from beneath my pillow, the familiar scent of the worn fabric immediately reminding me of the trailer I had left behind.

My mother's face flashed into my mind. Had she been thinking about us? Did she miss us at all? Would we see her again? If so, when?

The thoughts swirled in my head and mixed with a multitude of others as I drifted into a restless sleep — nightmares of evil aunts yelling and screaming and telling me to get out invaded my dreams.

When I woke in the middle of the night, I sat up in fright and wiped the sweat from my brow. Had the dream been an omen of sorts, a warning of what was ahead?

I tried to push the fear aside, but it remained with me and was still clinging to my insides when I woke the next morning.

CHAPTER THIRTEEN

Ali

As we walked toward the bus stop, we spotted Alexa and Tyler already standing there. Lucas ran ahead and started chatting animatedly with Tyler, probably about the play station game they were both so hooked on.

As we approached, I admired Alexa's clothing once again. She certainly had great taste in clothes. My next allowance was due soon, and I had been saving for some new shoes. I hoped we could go shopping together sometime.

"Hey, Alexa, I love your backpack!" I exclaimed, looking down at the bag by her feet. "Where did you get it?"

"Um, at the mall."

"Really? Which store? We got our school bags for Christmas. But yours is so much nicer."

She shrugged. "I can't remember the name of the store. I'll have to check with my aunt."

"Are you excited about today?" I prodded. "I was really nervous on my first day; I didn't know anyone."

"But you had Casey with you," Alexa countered.

Casey was frowning in my direction. She had already asked me not to blab everything out to Alexa, at least not until we got to know her a little better.

"Well, we'll both be with you today," I rushed on. "Let's just hope you end up in our class. If not, I'm going to beg Mrs. Jensen to move you. She's the principal, and she really likes us, so hopefully, she'll agree."

Alexa's eyes flickered to the badge on my sweater. "You're the school captain? Is that like a class president."

"Yeah," I grinned proudly. "And Casey's the vice-captain."

"Vice-captain?"

"Assistant captain," Casey explained with a shrug.

"We're both captains," I insisted. "There's no difference between the positions."

Casey shot me a look, and I knew what she was thinking.

I had the lead role and was given the most important jobs. But Casey had never wanted that position. And besides, she was the cheerleading captain for the second year in a row. Surely, that was enough?"

"I bet you're both smart," Alexa said with a knowing look. "Class presidents are always smart."

"She's the smart one," Casey pointed out.

"And she's the sporty one," I said, nudging Casey with my elbow. "She's the cheerleading captain as well."

Casey gave a modest shake of her head and stepped forward as the bus pulled up in front of us. I caught Alexa's nod of approval and hoped she wasn't sporty as well. I had more chance of her wanting to be my friend if she had similar interests to me.

It would be so much fun to include a fourth person in our close group at school. We had lots of friends, but the main group consisted of Casey, Brie, and me. Three was an odd number, plain and simple, and there was often someone left out. While there were plenty of other girls to pair up with, I wanted a best friend of my own. Even if Alexa only stayed temporarily, it would be cool if she liked me more. When we walked along the bus aisle, I nudged Casey forwards so we could all sit together on the rear seat.

When Alexa sat down, I grabbed the spot alongside her, and we chatted all the way to school.

CHAPTER FOURTEEN

Alexa

I had learned to tell lies from a young age. They weren't bad lies; that was what I told myself. But they usually saved me from further embarrassment. When kids asked me where I lived, I gave a vague answer, rarely admitting to the trailer park on the outskirts of town.

I still remembered the surprised gasp in my very first week of school. "You live in a trailer park? Is it a big trailer?"

No, it's a small one, it's old and dingy, and it leaks when it rains. That was the truthful answer, but it wasn't the one I gave. I simply shrugged and avoided mentioning it again. Even at that young age, I was already ranked quite low on the social ladder of the kids in my class. My shabby appearance was enough to put them off.

On the odd occasion that I was asked to hang out after school, I suggested we go to the other kids' houses or to the park or the mall, anywhere other than where I lived. I learned to keep secrets about my life; the details were my business and no one else's, which was why I didn't admit to not owning a phone when Casey asked for my number.

When the twins arrived at the bus shelter, I noticed they'd styled their hair very differently. One wore her hair in long waves, not as curly as the day before, and was dressed quite casually.

The other one wore a side ponytail and a stylish knitted sweater. I decided she had to be Ali. When she started speaking, I recognized her confident manner and was pleased I'd been able to figure out who was who.

When she asked where I'd bought my backpack, I decided to lie. "A store at the mall," I replied.

I didn't want to admit that my aunt had bought it. That would lead to embarrassing questions. "She bought your coat and your backpack as well? So generous of her. Did she buy you anything else?"

Yes, she did… she bought pretty much every decent piece of clothing I own… the jeans, the shirts, the sweaters, the jacket, the shoes. She even bought me new some new pajamas and some new underwear as well. And she chose it all without any input from me.

How embarrassing.

I had so many secrets tucked away, and I planned to keep them there. I just had to make sure Tyler did the same thing. What was the point in revealing the truth? Especially if we were going to be shipped off somewhere else where we'd have to start all over again. Why not live a lie while we could?

I was happy to act the part of a rich girl. Maybe for once in my life, I'd even be included in the cool group at school. I smirked at the thought.

Deep down, I knew that not all the cool kids were from wealthy families. A wealthy background wasn't necessary to be accepted into the cool crowd. But nice clothes were, along with pretty jewelry and maybe some make-up and accessories that made the cool kids stand out. Plus, a certain type of attitude.

I wasn't sure the twins had the typical cool kid attitude I was used to seeing. I was beginning to think they might be genuine people and not just interested in the clothes I was wearing. After all, Ali had seen me at my worst. I cringed at the memory of how I looked when I first met her in the driveway. Thinking back to that moment, I realized in a flash that she didn't even flinch at the way I looked. Instead of turning her nose up and walking away, she had invited me to hang out.

Was there a possibility we could become friends? Maybe I needed to let my past experiences go and think of this as a fresh start.

My thoughts began to run away with me, and I stopped to take a breath. Until I got to know the twins better, it was best to keep my distance. I could be ditched at any time, and I needed to be prepared for that. It had happened a few times in the past, and I didn't want to be made a fool of again.

My gaze landed on my brother, who was sitting further down the aisle, deep in conversation with Lucas. Those two had really hit it off. Hopefully, the kids in Tyler's class would be just as kind to him, and he'd have a really good first day.

At least he no longer had to wear shoes with holes in the toes and the sole of the left shoe flapping loosely underneath. It constantly caused him to trip, so much so that his teacher had wrapped some strong tape around the shoe to hold it together. That didn't stop his toes from poking out the top, or his feet from getting wet when it rained. As soon as Aunt Beth saw the state of those shoes, she pointed to the trash can and demanded that he dump them immediately.

In just two days, our lives had taken a dramatic turn, and I ran my hand through the slick tresses of my long hair, reveling in the silky feel rather than the matted mess I usually had to deal with each morning.

When the bus pulled into the school parking lot, I looked curiously out the window. I was about to step into more unfamiliar territory, and I knew it was best to be wary, but for the first time in a long time, I dared to hope for a positive outlook.

CHAPTER FIFTEEN

Casey

Ali continued to dominate Alexa's attention. During the ride to school, my twin barely took a breath, and I hardly got a chance to speak at all. Her manner was making me less interested in trying to repair things between us. I doubted she'd be interested in hearing what I had to say, anyway. After Alexa and her family left the night before, our new neighbor was all Ali could talk about. It was almost like the Meg scenario all over again.

Thoughts of Ali's best friend from her previous school still haunted me. Meg had wreaked havoc on our lives and almost tore Ali and me apart when she came to stay. As well, she had been determined to have Jake for herself. Her constant flirting went totally overboard, and she made my life miserable. Thankfully, Ali finally saw her for what she was. I just hoped Meg never weaseled her way into another visit. I couldn't stand the thought of it.

As for Alexa, she was nothing at all like the domineering Meg. She was quite the opposite. It was Ali who was suddenly obsessed and desperate for attention. I knew my twin pretty well, and I was aware she wanted Alexa's friendship to herself. The girl had only arrived two days earlier, but Ali had jumped right in and taken over.

Meanwhile, Ali's remarks the night before about Brie had surprised me. "Brie is Casey's best friend," she had said.

I didn't realize she felt that way. Brie and I had always included my twin. If anything, I sometimes worried that Brie was left out. It was tricky with three of us, especially if we had to partner up for class activities and cheerleading routines. Ali and I were also busy with school captain duties, and during those times, Brie hung out with other girls. We now had a fairly large friendship group, but Ali, Brie, and I were the closest. We'd become a tightknit threesome. At least, that was what I thought. Ali obviously had a different opinion.

I shook my head and sighed. It was all so complicated.

Sitting back in my seat, I watched Alexa with interest. After spending time with us the night before, she was opening up a bit more, compared to the previous day, when she acted a little overwhelmed and on edge. It was the same as my reaction when I first visited Ali's house. Her place was like a mansion in comparison to my home. I wasn't comfortable being there at all. It was also the moment I discovered how different our lives really were.

I was surprised by Alexa's response, though. I had never been inside her aunt and uncle's home, but the outside was certainly impressive. Surely she was used to luxury houses. But then, the modern interior of Ali's place was definitely an eye-opener. Ali's place. Would I ever think of it as my place too?

When we finally arrived at school, I looked out the window, hoping to see Jake. Spotting him straight away, I waved to catch his attention. His face widened into the smile that I adored. It never failed to melt my heart when I saw it.

He returned my wave, and I felt my heartbeat race as I stepped into the aisle. I loved the fact that he waited for me on Monday mornings. It was the one morning where both of us were free to meet, a perfect way to start the week.

As soon as I stepped onto the pavement, he walked over, his hand outstretched. I used to be shy about holding his hand at school, but it now felt the most natural thing in the world. Not that we always held hands, but when we did, it was special.

I turned to Ali and saw her eyes flicker over Jake's hand in mine. I offered her a smile, but hers was half-hearted in return.

I stifled a sigh. She would never admit to the fact, but my relationship with Jake bothered her. She was jealous of the attention he gave me. But what was I supposed to do? Stay away from him? I decided then and there to organize a group date for the following weekend: Ali, Mike, Brie, Wyatt, Jake, and me. We hadn't done that in so long. If Ali saw more of Mike, then my relationship with Jake wouldn't be an issue, I was sure of it.

"Hey, Ali," Jake said, shooting her a welcoming smile. "And... Alexa. I didn't know you were going to this school."

She gave him a shy nod. "Yeah, just while we're staying with our aunt and uncle."

"Cool!" Jake replied. "Do you know which class you're in? It'd be great if you were in ours."

Alexa's mouth curved into a wider smile. "Hopefully, I will be."

I felt a twinge of envy curl in my stomach. But I reminded myself that Jake was always super friendly. There was no harm in that, was there? Even so, I failed to push the uneasy sensation about Alexa's reaction aside.

"Come on, Alexa," Ali said, linking arms with her. "I'll show you where the office is."

Alexa gave Jake and me a quick wave. "I'll see you guys later."

I wasn't sure if I imagined it, but her eyes seemed to linger on Jake for a fraction longer than necessary.

Before I could dwell on that, Brie bounced over. "Hey, guys. Who's the new girl?" she asked, pointing in Alexa's direction.

"Our new neighbor," I explained. "Her name's Alexa. She's staying with her aunt and uncle. They live next door to us."

"Ali's pretty friendly with her already," Brie remarked.

"Yeah, I think she's found a new best friend."

Brie raised her eyebrows questioningly, and I shrugged. Before Brie could comment, Jake's friend, Sai, stepped up alongside us, and we spent a few minutes chatting together. When the two boys began discussing a new computer game, Brie and I were given a chance to focus on each other.

As we walked to our lockers, I filled her in on more details about Alexa. "I don't know how long she'll be staying," I added with a shrug. "I think her mom's very ill. So Alexa could be around for a while."

"Wow! Is she nice?"

"She's pretty quiet, but she seems really nice. I'll introduce you later."

"Sounds good," Brie said, then went on to tell me about her weekend. She'd been hanging out with Wyatt a lot and was hoping he'd soon ask her to be his girlfriend.

Distracted by the conversation with my friend, I pushed all thoughts of Alexa to the rear of my mind.

CHAPTER SIXTEEN

Alexa

I saw Jake from the bus window. It was impossible to miss him. His beaming smile was directed at Casey, and I could easily see how close the pair were; it was obvious even before we stepped off the bus and he reached for her hand. To be so adored by a boy as nice as Jake was hard to comprehend.

Once again, I wondered how Ali dealt with it all. No wonder she felt the need to compete. If I were her, I'd feel the same way. I still didn't know if she had a boyfriend, but I could tell by her friendly manner that it would only be a matter of time before I learned more about her.

Tyler and Lucas walked with us to the office. When we reached the counter, Lucas waved goodbye before running off to his classroom, which he said was situated on the other side of the school. Tyler's eyes were wide as he stood beside me. I could tell he was nervous. Thankfully, we were both in middle school, and I'd be close by if he needed me.

"Hi, Mrs. Gilmore," Ali said to the office lady, who wore a badge displaying her name. "This is Alexa and Tyler. They're new."

"Ah, yes, the Morrison siblings. Hello, Alexa. Hi, Tyler." She offered each of us a warm smile. "We were expecting you. Your aunt called to enroll you on Friday." She turned back to Ali and gave her a pleased nod. "Great to see you helping out some new students, Ali."

"We're actually neighbors," Ali replied. "Their aunt and uncle live next door to my family."

"Well, what a coincidence," Mrs. Gilmore remarked as she consulted her computer screen.

"Alexa and I were hoping she might be in our class," Ali prompted, leaning over the counter and glancing at the screen.

"It just so happens you're in luck," Mrs. Gilmore said.

"Really?" Ali let out a small squeal and grinned at me.

"Yes. Alexa has been placed in the same class as you and Casey."

I sucked in a relieved breath as I took in the news.

"And Tyler, you're in Mr. Maxwell's class in Block B, room 25. Here are your locker combinations, guys." She handed Tyler and me a slip of paper each, then looked at Ali. "Can you direct them, please, Ali?"

"Yes, of course. We'll take Tyler to his locker first. Then we'll walk him to his room so he can meet his teacher."

"Thank you, Ali." Mrs. Gilmore gave her another pleased nod. "Alexa and Tyler, welcome to our school. I hope you both enjoy your time here."

"Thanks," I replied, collecting my backpack from the floor by my feet and following Ali along the corridor.

"She's so nice," I said to Ali as I slung my bag over my shoulder. "So much friendlier than the office lady at our other school. She's a witch. Everyone's scared of her, even the teachers."

"Really?" Ali laughed. "Mrs. Gilmore's always been nice to me."

"Probably because you're a school captain," I said, pointing to her badge.

Ali smiled and shrugged away my comment. She was thrilled we were in the same class, and I was feeling the same way. If only Tyler were so lucky.

As we walked, I caught my brother's anxious

expression. "It'll be okay, Tyler. I'm sure there'll be some nice kids in your class. You'll make new friends easily."

"Everyone loves new kids," Ali assured him. "On my first day, I was swamped with kids wanting to be my friend."

That's because you're you. I thought to myself. Ali and Casey were different from Tyler and me. Their friendly personas, plus the way they looked, made a great impression straight away. I wondered if I could learn from Ali. Perhaps I should try to be less standoffish; maybe then I could make a similar impression.

I was so scared of rejection, though. If everyone learned the truth about me, everything would change. The clothes were a camouflage, and the real me was underneath. Would the other kids see through the disguise and realize that?

I was also concerned about my brother. At times, he struggled to control his temper. But if he got into any fights, as he had done a few times in recent months at our other school, our aunt would freak out. And that would be the end for us.

I warned Tyler that morning on our way to the bus stop. "We can't mess up, Tyler. Any problems, and she'll kick us out."

He knew who and what I was talking about. I didn't need to explain. So far, he'd been a perfect little angel. But it had only been two days. What would the weeks ahead bring?

I chewed on my lip as I walked, hoping for the best.

CHAPTER SEVENTEEN

Ali

When Alexa and I approached her locker, I huffed in dismay. Of all people, Ronnie Miller had a locker right next to Alexa's. I steeled myself as we neared her. "Don't you have hallway duties this morning, Ronnie?"

"No, I don't, and besides, what business is it of yours?" she scoffed.

I gritted my teeth and turned to my new friend. "Alexa, this is Ronnie. She's one of the hallway monitors. Just be careful. She loves reporting kids to the principal, so make sure you don't do anything wrong, or she'll add you to her list."

I ignored Ronnie's scowl and pointed to Alexa's locker. "This one's yours. I'll be back as soon as I sort out my books."

I was worried about Ronnie. It would be so typical for her to try to get the new girl on side; especially now she knew I was Alexa's friend. I wouldn't normally let Ronnie get to me, but lately her bullying had spiked to a new level, and I'd had enough. Ignoring her didn't work. The only way to deal with the likes of Ronnie Miller was to stand up to her.

Just as I reached my locker, I saw Mrs. Jensen striding down the corridor. She locked her eyes on me. "Good morning, Ali. I need you and Casey to come to my office straight away. I have a job for you, girls. I'll let Ms. Harris know you'll be late to class."

My mouth dropped open in protest. Really? Of all mornings, she had to pick that one?

She gave me a sharp look. "Is there a problem, Ali?"

"Um, no," I stammered. "I'll find Casey, and we'll be right there."

"Please be quick," she said as she stepped away.

I looked back in Alexa's direction, where I could see her and Ronnie chatting. The pair broke into laughter, and I clenched my teeth with annoyance as I shoved my backpack into my locker.

Hurrying back to Alexa, I tapped her on the shoulder. "Casey and I have to go to the office. Mrs. Jensen, the principal, needs us to help her with something. But our classroom is just down the hall. Room 18. I'll see you there a bit later, okay?"

"I can show you where it is, Alexa," Ronnie piped up. "Just stick with me, you'll be fine."

She turned to me with a smirk, and I gave her a seething glare before rushing off to find my twin. Mrs. Jensen wouldn't be pleased if we kept her waiting.

CHAPTER EIGHTEEN

Alexa

I could see that Ali and Ronnie didn't get on. I caught Ali's annoyed expression, and her reaction surprised me. I hadn't expected her to be so rude. Weren't class presidents normally goody-two-shoes type people? Ronnie certainly didn't hold back either, though Ali put her in her place with the hallway monitor taunt.

Hallway monitor? How did she end up with that job? At my other school, the hallway monitors were the most hated kids in the school. It was their role to report kids, and the ones who had that authority usually took advantage. By the sound of Ali's warning, Ronnie was no different. But if she was as bad as Ali had said, perhaps I needed to get on her good side.

Surprisingly, I found her chatty and helpful and super nice. When she led me along the corridor, she asked me a few questions about where I was from. I gave her the same spiel as I'd given the twins, but she didn't question it. The lack of details didn't seem to bother her at all.

As we walked, I was conscious of several kids staring my way.

"It's because you're new," Ronnie whispered in my ear. "They'll probably all want to be your friend. But I can let you know which ones to stay away from." She gave me a conspiratorial nudge with her elbow. "See that girl over there," she nodded in the direction of a brown-haired girl hovering by the doorway. "She's the biggest loser in the whole class. Her name's Samantha, and she's seriously weird! She likes to be called Sammi, S-A-Double M-I. If you don't spell it correctly, she freaks out."

The girl held up her fingers in a peace symbol as I passed her. Her smile was friendly enough, but the peace sign was an odd thing to do.

"Told you," Ronnie giggled as we entered the room.

She led me over to the teacher's desk. "Hi, Ms. Harris, this is Alexa. She's new to the school."

Ms. Harris stood up from her seat and smiled. "Hello, Alexa. I was told you'd be arriving today. Lovely to meet you."

"Hello," I murmured quietly. Ali had said she was nice, but I wasn't sure Casey felt the same way. I guess I'd soon form my own opinion.

She walked over to the far wall and pointed to a desk. "I've set up a desk for you right here."

"Ms. Harris," Ronnie interrupted politely. "I was wondering if Alexa could sit next to me? Holly's going to be away all week, so the desk next to mine is free for now."

Ms. Harris nodded her head. "That's a great idea, Ronnie. That way, you can help Alexa settle in. But when Holly returns, Alexa will have to move."

"Okay, that's fine. Thanks, Ms. Harris." Ronnie quipped and motioned for me to follow her. She pointed to the desk beside hers. "You can sit here."

I slid into the seat just as the room began to fill with kids. Amongst the group was a girl who looked familiar. As I watched her walk across the room, I recalled seeing her in a photo in the twins' bedroom. Casey's best friend... Brie, I thought her name was.

As soon as she saw me, her eyes lit up in recognition as if she knew who I was. My presence in the room also sparked the attention of the girls around her.

"Do we have a new girl?"

"Is she new?"

"Wow, a new student."

I could hear their murmurs as they drew nearer.

"Oh, not fair. Why can't we get a new boy for a change?" a tall olive-skinned boy moaned as he walked by.

Within seconds, my desk was surrounded as curious kids wanted to know who I was and where I had come from. Before I had a chance to speak, Ronnie stepped in. "Her name's Alexa. It's her first day. So give her some space."

"Who made you the boss?" one of the girls scoffed before walking away.

Ronnie sniggered in my ear. "They're all such drama queens."

I smirked back, pleased to avoid all the questions. It was much easier that way. Although I was surprised by their reactions. I had never been an attraction before. At least, not in a good way. I flicked a strand of hair from my eyes and lifted my chin, a thread of confidence winding through me. This time, the confidence felt real, not something fake that I sprayed on as a protective layer. When the bell rang, and Ms. Harris introduced me to the class, I was able to keep my head high, rather than trying to crawl into an invisible shell where I could hide, which was normally the case when I was singled out.

I wondered how my brother was going and hoped he was getting the same reception. *Just be nice to the other kids, Tyler, and you'll be fine.* I sent a silent prayer through the airwaves, hoping it would connect with him. He was a great kid, but he could explode at the drop of a hat. If he could keep his anger under control, everything would be okay.

I caught Casey's friend, Brie, looking my way, and when our eyes connected, she offered me a friendly smile. I smiled back and then returned my attention to the teacher who was asking us to take out our spelling books. She passed around some worksheets, and when I saw the crossword and other activities, I stared at them in dismay. I had never been good at spelling, and I chewed on my lip as I looked it over.

From the corner of my eye, I glanced at Ronnie's sheet. She'd dived straight in and was having no trouble at all. I kept a discreet eye on her work and filled the boxes on my crossword with the same letters as Ronnie's.

After a while, she must have noticed because she moved her arm so I could see her work. "This crossword is pretty tricky. You can copy mine if you want. But I can't guarantee it's right," she chuckled quietly.

I gave her a grateful smile and continued copying the letters. I was good at math, in fact, I loved working with numbers, but English was my least favorite subject.

"You're a smart girl, Alexa," my teachers had tried to reassure me time and time again. "You just need to work on your spelling. The more reading you do, the better you'll become."

But I didn't like reading, and there were very few books in the school library that interested me, so I rarely borrowed anything.

Thankfully, Ronnie was more than willing to help me with the activities. Perhaps I really had lucked out by sitting alongside her. Although, when Holly came back, whoever Holly was, I knew I'd have to move.

When I noticed Ali and Casey entering the room, I watched as they approached the teacher. "Sorry we're late, Ms. Harris. Mrs. Jensen needed our help in the office."

"That's fine, girls," Ms. Harris replied. "Please take your seats and get started on the worksheet.

The two girls turned to face the class, and both pairs of eyes landed on me before flickering to Ronnie. The surprise on each of their faces was the same.

Ali's expression quickly turned to a grimace.

CHAPTER NINETEEN

Ali

Why was Alexa sitting in Holly's desk next to Ronnie? And where was Holly? I scanned the room but couldn't see her anywhere.

It was so typical of Ronnie to take over. She was such a snake when she wanted to be. I remembered how nice she was to me when I first arrived at the school. I was a new girl and a novelty, one she was eager to get to know. She barely knew me, but that didn't stop her from inviting me to her birthday party. It was a sleep-over, and at the time, I couldn't believe my luck. But it didn't take me long to discover the real Ronnie lurking underneath.

When Ronnie's true colors shone through, I learned to see her for what she was… a vindictive bully. She even preyed upon my friend, Meg, when she came to stay with me. And that led to so much drama, something I wanted to forget.

As the morning dragged by, I darted several glances in Alexa's direction. We had a double period of English, followed by History, all taught by Ms. Harris, which meant we were stuck in our seats for the entire time. Alexa smiled and waved to me at one point, but most of the time, she was too busy whispering to Ronnie to even notice me. What were they talking about anyway? And why was she opening up to Ronnie?

Ronnie was a chameleon. She could lay on the nice girl charm when she wanted to. She'd fooled me, and she had also fooled Meg. And now she was digging her claws into Alexa as well. I couldn't blame Alexa. Until she grew to know the real Ronnie, she'd be bewitched by her spell.

When the bell for recess finally rang, I jumped out of my seat and shuffled quickly over to Alexa. "Hey, Alexa. Do you want to hang out during the break? I can show you around the school."

Ronnie linked a possessive arm through Alexa's as if she were her best friend. "I've already promised Alexa that I'll do that. Don't worry, Ali, I'll take good care of her."

Pushing on Alexa's arm, she steered her toward the classroom door. Alexa turned to me with an apologetic shrug. "I'll catch up with you later, Ali." With a slight wave of her hand, she disappeared from the room, leaving me to stare after her.

"Ronnie hasn't wasted any time," Casey grumbled from beside me.

I looked at her and rolled my eyes. "She's such a troublemaker. I can't stand her."

"You know I feel exactly the same way." Casey offered me a sympathetic smile and wrapped a sisterly arm around my shoulder. "Let's go out to the courtyard. I have a plan for next weekend. We should all hang out... the boys and us. We haven't done that for ages."

"A triple date? Sounds like a great idea," Brie said, stepping up alongside us.

Casey wrapped her other arm around Brie, and together we marched from the room. I decided I'd catch up with Alexa later and warn her before Ronnie got her hooks in too deep. As I focused on my twin's idea, my frustration over Ronnie faded. A group date was a wonderful suggestion. Mike always agreed to those, and I nodded happily at the thought of seeing him again.

"I'm just going to the bathroom," Brie said as we passed the bathroom door. "I'll meet you guys outside."

"Okay. But don't take long," Casey chirped. "We

have lots to talk about."

As we walked, Casey shared a joke that Brie had told her in class, and I was immediately in fits of laughter. I couldn't remember the last time we had joked together. Casey's smile told me she was thinking the same thing. Our connection bubbled to the surface, and it felt good to take a step back and enjoy being a twin, rather than begrudging my sister's presence all the time. I was guilty of that, and it had to stop.

We settled in our favorite spot in the corner of the courtyard and pulled out our lunch boxes, each of us munching on the delicious home-baked banana bread that Grandma Ann had brought by the afternoon before. As we chatted about Casey's plan for the weekend and tossed around ideas, all my concerns about Alexa and Ronnie flew from my mind. Maybe this could be a fresh beginning for my twin and me and help us get back to how we used to be. I knew it was up to me to make an effort to put aside my jealous streak and perfectionist attitude. That would be a really great start.

I was about to broach the subject with Casey, maybe even apologize for the way I'd been behaving, when Brie appeared, her face flushed.

"Where have you been?" Casey asked her. "You took forever."

Brie inhaled a deep breath then blew it out again as she regarded each of us.

"What's wrong?" I asked. Brie was acting weird, and I frowned at her questioningly.

She drew in another breath, and then the words spilled out. "When I was in the bathroom, I heard Ronnie talking to Alexa. They came in just after me, and I recognized Ronnie's voice. They didn't know I was in there."

"What did they say?" Casey prodded impatiently.

"Ronnie was talking about both of you. She was saying some horrible things."

"Like what?" I blurted out, my stomach dropping.

"She was telling Alexa all about your past… how you were separated at birth and all that stuff. She told Alexa your mom didn't want you, Ali. And that was why she gave you away."

Casey looked at me and huffed in disgust. Ronnie had said the same thing to me before, and now she was saying it to Alexa. That girl was unbelievable. "What else did she say?"

Brie bit her lip, reluctant to continue.

"What, Brie?" Casey pushed. "You have to tell us."

Brie dashed a look between us and sighed. "She told Alexa that as soon as Ali's adopted mom died, your birth mom stepped in. She called her a gold digger and said she only married your dad for his money."

My mouth dropped open as I processed Brie's words.

I stared aghast at my twin. Ronnie was the queen of gossip, but this was worse than any gossip we'd ever heard her spread before. It was personal, it was cruel, and it was all lies. Was she spreading this around the school? Who else had she told?

Several words filled my head to describe her. Words I would never say aloud, but in Ronnie's case, I couldn't avoid bringing them to mind.

My head spun wildly. As well as the gossip, there was more to worry about. If Alexa became friends with Ronnie, what would happen then? Would she turn against us too?

I sensed the worst was yet to come, and I was at a loss for how to prevent it.

Little did I know, however, Ronnie was the least of my concerns. There was something much bigger in store for us that no one, not even Ronnie could ever have been prepared for.

Look out for the next book in this series.
The New Girl – Book 2: A Whole New Dilemma

And be sure to follow me on Instagram @katrinakahler
or subscribe to my website... katrinakahler.com
so you can stay up to date on all my new releases.

I hope you've enjoyed the story so far!
If you liked it and you can spare the time, I'd really
appreciate a review.
Thanks so much!
Katrina x

If you haven't read the Twins series yet, the books are available on amazon, in combined sets, at a discounted price.

Twins – Part One: Books 1 to 3

Here are some more of my books. I hope you enjoy these stories too.

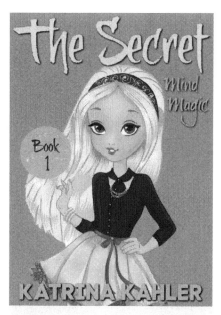

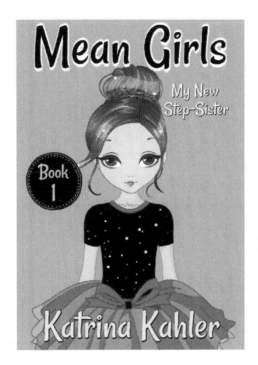

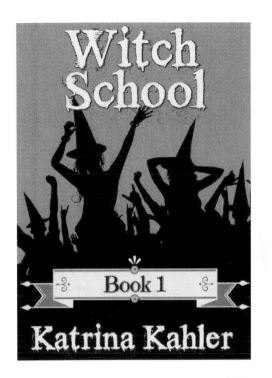

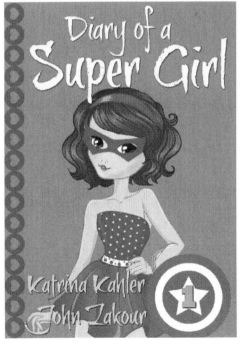